# GOD'S COUNTRY

KERRY HADLEY-PRYCE was born in the Black Country. She worked nights in a Wolverhampton petrol station before becoming a secondary school teacher. She wrote her first novel, *The Black Country*, whilst studying for an MA in Creative Writing at the Manchester Writing School at Manchester Metropolitan University, for which she gained a distinction and was awarded the Michael Schmidt Prize for Outstanding Achievement 2013–14. She is currently a PhD student at Manchester Metropolitan University, researching Psychogeography and Black Country Writing. *God's Country* is her third novel.

# KERRY HADLEY-PRYCE

# GOD'S COUNTRY

SALT

CROMER

PUBLISHED BY SALT PUBLISHING 2023

2 4 6 8 10 9 7 5 3 1

First published in Great Britain in 2023 by
Salt Publishing Ltd
12 Norwich Road, Cromer, Norfolk NR27 0AX United Kingdom

www.saltpublishing.com

Salt Publishing Limited Reg. No. 5293401

A CIP catalogue record for this book is available from the British Library

ISBN 978 1 78463 265 6 (Paperback edition)
ISBN 978 1 78463 266 3 (Electronic edition)

Typeset in Neacademia by Salt Publishing

Printed and bound in Great Britain by Clays Ltd, Elcograf S.p.A

*To my family*

SHE'LL SAY SHE wants to tell you this story, and in the act of telling it, she knows she'll probably leave some gaps, but in the act of you reading it, you'll give it shape. And maybe you might want to consider this: *Can you imagine your whole life being about the worst thing you ever did?*

Think about that now.

※

They travelled up here by car but an accident on the M5 had already added almost two hours to the journey. A car had burst into flames. Two people had died at the scene, apparently. Alison will say how she was uncomfortable, thirsty, needed the loo. She had a headache that was getting worse, and had forgotten to bring any pain killers. They seemed to have been at a standstill in the fast lane for ages. Guy turned the engine off.

'Five hours it would have taken us if we'd come on the train,' he said. He was jumpy, pink, blotchy – his face and neck. Alison will say it was always like he could read her mind. 'So don't say anything . . .'

'Well it's taken us more than that now.' She would have been pointing at the clock on the dashboard, then pointing at the traffic motionless in front of them. 'Got to be six, seven hours now, probably. And we're not even . . . I mean, where are we exactly?'

'Alison, I looked,' he said. 'I checked. There are no direct trains to the Black Country from our place, I told you.'

He'll have been doing that thing with his mouth, letting

his top teeth slide over the bottom lip repeatedly. Not quite biting. She'll have been able to see it getting sore, his lip. And calling her 'Alison,' calling her by her full name, she'll say now, was something he only ever did when he was annoyed, agitated.

She'll say she remembers him switching the radio off. They must have heard the same news, how many times? And the weather forecast. Expect snow, they kept being told, ice on untreated roads, expect cold.

She'll say she remembers Guy going on and on, saying, 'We'd have had to catch buses, God knows how many trains. We'd have been walking and waiting, hanging about. I told you. It was four or five changes at least.' He counted them off on his fingers, so she'll say. 'Six or seven different trains, probably. And it's freezing out. It is, look at it.'

He was wound up, and he was exaggerating, of course. She'll say, she'll explain, this is what he does when he's nervous, when he's anxious. She'll tell how he started the engine and the warmish air that blasted out from the vent onto her face smelled of petrol and smoke, how she looked out of the side window at a child urinating on the grassy bank just the other side of the hard shoulder, how a woman standing next to him smoked a cigarette and gazed now and then out at the line of traffic ahead.

'Stressful enough as it is.' Guy said this, she'll say so.

'Where are we, anyway?' Alison said. She'll tell how she opened her window, suddenly needing air.

'I dunno,' he said, and she'll tell how flustered he was. 'How should I know? Nobody knows. Tewkesbury? Evesham? The Seventh Circle of Hell? Christ knows.'

She'll say she sighed, at him, wanted to say something. He had no particular right to snap at her, not after what she'd

2

been through. But he didn't know then, did he? And he never would, actually. She'll say she thought then about telling him outright, there and then. But the woman and the child outside scampered back down the bank towards the car ahead of them. Before he got in, the child looked straight at her, Alison. She'll say she noticed his trousers were damp around the crotch. She stuck her tongue out, wrinkled her nose at him, watched as a look of disgust crossed his face and the woman ushered him into the back seat of the car.

Guy said something like, 'Horrible kid.' And thumped the steering wheel. 'Come. On!' he yelled at the lines of traffic ahead of him.

Alison will say she remembers straining to see beyond the cars ahead. 'What does that sign up there say?' she said. She'll have been squinting, perhaps she'll have thought she had a migraine coming on, on top of everything. She'll tell how she read the sign aloud: 'Worcester? Thirty-five?'

She'll say she remembers she said it for something to say, to break the possibility of an argument or a silence, or a truth emerging, but she said it like she'd never said the words before, like she'd never even seen the words before. Guy must have noticed how West Country she'd suddenly become, saying 'Worcester' like a right yokel.

'Well, that's where we are then, obviously, isn't it?' he said, and she'll say she felt, rather than saw, him flash a glance at her. 'Worcester, *twenty*-five, actually.' And he tutted, shook his head, said, 'You need new specs.'

'Sorry.' She'll have said it under her breath, and she'll say she remembers how she took off her glasses, started cleaning them with the corner of her cardigan.

Beside them, in the middle lane, she'll tell how there was a young man wearing a baseball cap sitting, quite relaxed, in his Audi, engine off, smoking a cigarette, his elbow pointing out of his open window like a weapon, smoke wafting straight in through Alison's open window.

'Do you want to close your window?' Guy said. He was talking to Alison, but the young man obviously heard, turned to look at them. She'll say she wondered what he was thinking, where he was going, this Audi driver, whether he had a girlfriend, children, where he was from. She'll tell how she watched him smoking that cigarette, inhaling the smoke like it was the way to ecstasy, and gently breathing it out in perfectly formed smoke rings. She'll admit to looking at the way his mouth moved, at his perfectly sculpted beard. She most likely thought she saw a twinkle in his eyes, at her. It was a performance, she'll say she thought, for her, and she wanted to applaud him. She will have been in another world, watching that young man when Guy touched her arm and she saw, when she looked, a bit of something, grit or some such, in the corner of his eye. She'll say she thought about just flicking it out with her little finger, poking it out, but didn't. She knew, of course, that he was tired, both of them were, but he looked it. She'll describe the big dark hollows beneath his eyes, how they seemed to have been drawn there, how his lip was dark pink and sore from not-quite-biting, and how he'd nicked his chin shaving that morning because it was so early and dark when they got up. She'll say, just then, she wondered what he'd look like with a beard, or breathing perfectly formed smoke rings. Perhaps that's when she first had the idea. I don't suppose we'll know now. Anyway. In truth, they'd both been working too hard, the last thing they needed was this trip, really, especially in the circumstances. This was why – one of the reasons why – she hadn't told him what she'd done. There's only so much stress a person can take. Guy had

4

already missed a deadline at work and she'd been through this – this situation – before, she hadn't told him then, either, so really, she'll say she knew she ought to be resting, feet up, or something. And she would have been, if they hadn't had to come here.

'Your window. Do you want to close it?'

She'll say she remembers he said again, and he motioned towards the Audi driver.

'It's a bit stuffy in here with the heating on full blast,' she said.

'It's cold,' Guy said. 'And a bit smoky.' And he coughed, he forced a cough – she'll remember that.

The Audi driver caught on to what was being said. He looked at her as if she was prey of some kind to him and she'll say she quite liked that.

But she closed her window, and the sound of it, and the speed of it seemed somehow ridiculous, seemed to create a vacuum straight away. It wasn't lost on the Audi driver, she'll say she remembers that, and he narrowed his eyes and breathed out a cirrus of smoke in her direction. She was smiling, she knew she was, and she'll admit he was good looking, but when she realised Guy was giving her one of his looks, she said, 'God.' She'll say she said it quietly, aimed it at the Audi driver, and she waved her hands about in a kind of performance. 'Give us all cancer, why don't you?'

Guy looked at her, and she'll say she knew that look well. She'll tell how she rubbed her fingertips lightly and briefly on the outside of his thigh.

'Oh, Christ, Guy . . .' she said. 'I'm sorry, I shouldn't have said that.'

Guy sighed. He would have sighed instead of saying anything.

'That was thoughtless, me saying something like that,' she said. 'I'm really sorry.'

Ahead of them, she'll say the traffic had just begun to move. They would have been able to see it begin to shift, like the vertebrae of an enormous monster that they were part of, and up ahead, the blue lights of the fire engines, the police cars.

'I really am,' Alison said, and she would have been squeezing his thigh, and her breath would have been chemical with thirst. 'I'm an idiot for saying that.'

She'll say now, she just needed to keep him on-side.

Don't feel sorry for her.

She'll tell how she remembers Guy finding first gear, saying, 'Thank Christ for that,' and how he was concentrating on the horizon, leaning forward, seeming to want to push forward physically. She would have taken hold of his fingers if she could have, if she could have brought herself to, that is, but both his hands were on the wheel, and it was late, and nobody wants to be late for their own brother's funeral, especially when it's your twin brother.

&

They stopped at Strensham Services. She likes motorway service stations, Alison does. She likes the transience of it all, the brutalism of the look of them, the strange grace of that, the way lives collide in a way they wouldn't, couldn't, elsewhere, the possibility of chance, the movement. She likes the fairground quality of the layout, the way the food smells, the trancelike look on the faces of the staff, unlike staff anywhere else.

Guy was pulling up at the pump, she'll say, when she asked him, 'Do we have time for a coffee?'

She might say he hesitated, that she couldn't tell if it was impatience. It probably was. 'I thought you said you needed the loo,' he said and he got out of the car and walked towards the kiosk, his legs clearly stiff from driving for so long, his shoulders already anyway made round by working at a computer all day, his back much more hunched, she noticed, and just for a moment, she'll say she saw him as she thought he might become: jaded, a little haggard, like someone who does physical work of some kind – hard, physical work.

She'll talk about how the sun suddenly glinted off something – something on the awning of the forecourt or a window – and it was like the flash of a camera, momentarily blinding, and she'll say that when she looked at him, the way it coloured him, Guy, he seemed to be merging, even then, with the elements of this place, as if he'd been the missing component. She'll say it made her want to close her eyes, at least.

There was a queue for the Ladies, there always is. And there were end-of-line Christmas decorations next to Valentine's cards in the shop there and she'll say she watched as a young couple considered buying a giant inflatable heart. Everything seemed so expensive to her. Garish posters behind scratched Perspex advertised cheap, fast food. Buy one, get one free. A woman wearing orange workwear strolled by, eyes down, pushing an oversized broom. Alison will say she noticed this woman was wearing three, no, four gold rings at least on the fingers of one hand.

She'll say that the queue moved quickly, but the cubicle she chose had no lock and she had to sit with her foot against the door. She'd been desperate, and it seemed to take an age for her to finish. Someone tried to push the door, but she managed to hold it closed, just. Then she'll say she stood up a bit too quickly and everything went flickery and she had to hold on to the toilet roll holder until the feeling passed, and then the sanitary bin was full and she had to prod hers down into it. She'd leaked a bit, and there was blood, dried, on the crotch of her jeans and then there was no soap in any of the dispensers, and the water was either very cold or very hot. She'll say she swallowed a palm-full of water that tasted of metal, and when she came out, into the concourse, the inflatable heart had gone, and she recognised the young man she'd seen in the Audi earlier, paying for something at the till. He didn't seem to see her. She bought the last two packs of pain-killers on the shelf. Overpriced, she'll say she thought.

Outside, the forecourt was full of cars, despite the price of the petrol. Apparently, she noticed a people carrier at the opposite pump, full of children, most of them complaining in sing-song high-pitched voices she'd sometimes heard Guy use when he was tired or particularly pissed off. Trying to work out what they were saying was like trying, and failing, to tune into a radio station, so she'll say. The youngest child, little more than a baby, even seemed to be crying with the same intonation. In another car, she'll say how she could hear a couple talking. 'We ought to just leave now,' one of them said. And 'Things Can Only Get Better' faded out as they drove off onto the sliproad.

She'll say she noticed the air here was different from their home. Gritty, she thought, dirty and dampish and heavy with something. She'd have wondered whether it was healthy or not, or whether she was just imagining it. She'll say she felt it, tasted it, that sweetish bitterness of something prehistoric as if the place was shrouded in something, preserved by something. Maybe she thought it's the air quality that carries sound differently, making this odd pitch in the voice, like helium might because she'll say the sound from the children

8

in the people carrier seemed relentless. She felt herself becoming agitated, she'll say she actually felt herself frowning. Do something, she was thinking. Why doesn't the parent do something? She'll say she thought of the name: Black Country, and all the connotations, and everything she'd heard about it, everything Guy had told her. Grit and damp was what she'd expected, of course. She'd expected an area drizzled with grey or sepia, perhaps very little difference between day and night, she'd pictured people round-shouldered with manual labour and the odd sound of distant clanging metal or blasts from furnaces somewhere. She'd imagined calculated rows of Victorian terraced houses, non-stop. She'd thought there'd be ancient factories, quaint, if nothing else, now that there was not so much manufacturing. She'd packed thick jumpers because she'd imagined it to be especially cold here. Of course, it is. But she'd never been here before, and Guy had left, how many years ago? Fifteen? And he hadn't been back. She'll say she'd begun to think he might have been making it up, this Black Country of his, she'd never been able to find it on a map, and she hadn't expected to feel anything like what she was feeling about being here.

And she'll tell this: as she stood on the edge of the forecourt, an aeroplane flew overhead, low, from Birmingham airport, she guessed, and made the windows of the cars, and of the kiosk, seem to shiver, but it seemed to give her, she'll say, a sense that if she wanted to, she could leave this place, that it would be possible to board a plane like that and go anywhere. If she wanted to, when she wanted to. Guy, when she looked, was standing in a queue inside the kiosk, watching her. It made her feel odd, unsettled, being looked at like that. She'll tell how her headache was developing, she thought, a throb above her left eye, and there were floaters that were messing with her vision. To her, just then, Guy appeared to be swathed in smoke. There was a sense of hearing things in 3D, of actually apprehending this place here differently. She will have wished for water or coffee so she could take the pain-killers, she will have wished she could just have a lie down, she'd perhaps have felt better then. She'll say this is what she'd thought, just then.

Inside the car, to her, she'll say it smelt of heat and sweat, and of Guy, the smell of him, his aftershave or whatever, which clung to everything. She closed her eyes and saw patterns in red and black. She must have fallen asleep immediately because Guy opening the door was a shock. She felt herself rearing up, she'll say, straightening up, pulling tight the muscles in her legs, her back.

'I don't know what this'll be like,' he said as he sat down, handing her a coffee cup. 'I put a load of sugar in it to mask the taste, but I bet it still tastes like shit.'

When she took it from him, both of them noticed she was trembling, she'll say she's sure of that.

'Lack of food,' she said, because she just didn't want him to ask any questions, not just then.

That little piece of grit was still there, in the corner of his eye, she noticed. If she could just hook it out with her fingernail.

'Ali,' Guy said, and he sighed. She'll say she remembers feeling the blood rushing to her face, feeling herself stiffen, she'll say now she felt like the whole of the Black Country was watching them, watching her. 'You didn't have to come here,' he said. He whispered it.

'I wanted to,' she said.

'No-one *wants* to come here,' he said. 'Especially . . . *here*.'

She'll say she remembers how he sat, looking straight ahead.

It was a migraine she was getting, likelihood was that this aura she could already see would become a thunderous pain. Already the kiosk had disappeared from her view, slurried by some false image, some false light or dark that was going on in her head. To her, just then, there was smoke everywhere.

'No-one ever *wants* to come here,' Guy said, again and he wasn't smiling.

The people carrier pulled away from the pump opposite. She couldn't see or hear any of the children. It was as if they'd vanished, or, she thought, had been left in lost property, or had been dumped in the motorway services, left playing on the fruit machines or the computer games, or given away, or sold, or left to run in a panic across the carriageway. It was as if they'd been surgically removed. To her that's how it will have seemed, and she let her hand hover above her own belly for a second, like a magician performing a disappearing trick.

'Look, I know,' Guy said without looking at her. 'It's been hard.'

'Hard for *you*,' she said, quickly. 'He was your brother.'

Outside, the wind like an off-chord being struck time and again made it feel like they might have been right about the snow.

She took two pain-killers with a mouthful of coffee. It was scalding hot, still, but it was the gathering pain in her head, behind her eye, that was all she could feel. She'll say. Perhaps that's all she wanted to feel.

'You OK?' Guy said.

'Yeh, fine,' she said.

She'll say she imagined the migraine as a clump of something red, irregular or with branches or roots like tentacles. Some kind of toxic plant, say, like a triffid, that was capable of growing and creeping and burrowing into her brain. And she'd imagined the pain-killers as a bunch, no, an army, of soldiers, with flame-throwers, searing away the thickening stems with jets of fire – she could hear them doing it – of them scorching out roots until all that would be left was damage. Her poor damaged brain. This was on the journey from the motorway into the Black Country. Every now and then she closed her eyes and imagined her brain like the surface of wild earth, and all the little footprints melded into a mess of dryness, of ash. Whenever they stopped at junctions or traffic lights, she jolted herself awake, thinking they were there, that they'd arrived at the farm – because it was the farm they were heading for: Guy's childhood home. Sometimes, there were live digital screens on bus stops, flickering pixelated images of far-off places, or commodities nobody really needs. Against the jaundiced light, it all looked degraded, out of place. Guy woke her once saying something about the Google Street View car, prowling down a street of terraced houses in front of them. Later, she heard him say, 'We're there.' She heard him sigh it. She can't have realised how very tired she was, how she must have fallen asleep again. She'll say how she noticed the two dots of coffee she'd spilt on her jeans seemed to be blooming before her eyes, clumping into a philtrum as if about to form the shape of a human face. It made her shiver, and she put her hand over that. Guy noticed her doing it as he changed gear, he must have, because she'll say she remembers him saying, 'Don't go worrying about that. Nobody at the farm'll notice.'

He called it 'The Farm', Guy did, whenever he talked about his life before, whenever he mentioned where his family lived, which, anyway, wasn't often. Alison will say now that, at first, she'd thought that was strange, that he never called it 'home', it was always either 'The Farm' or 'there'. Of course, she knows why now.

The car was struggling, or so it seemed to her, or perhaps Guy was deliberately driving very, very slowly. It was a rough uphill lane, sand or clay, because that's what this place is made of. There were potholes, deep ones, that made it feel dangerous and made the car move unpredictably, like everything was being knocked out of kilter. And when it came into view, the house, the farm, it looked like it was perched on the side of a volcano. That's how Alison will describe it. She'll say she was struck by the blocks of blackened stone it was made of, the layers, and how they looked. Not brick. Like a house made of coal. Nothing that she'd ever seen before, but strangely impressive. She'll say now that a quote came to mind, something from Heaney: 'The sump-life of the place like old chain oil.' It was like the poetry came at her, just looking at this farm here, just looking at this place. And, she'll say now, it seemed to her then, if anything, like a good place to die.

What she'll say she remembers is that between the house and an old caravan, there was strung a longish washing line on which there were billowing sheets and towels, and on the most exposed side of the house there was scaffolding that looked, she'll say, like a strange puzzle. As they approached, she'd have been able to see lines of footfall alongside the dry-stone wall. Later, she'd be told it was called a desire path. And the wall, ancient looking, broken and loose in places, looked experimental – it still does. And an old Land Rover was parked skewiff across the drive.

Guy stopped the car a little distance from the farm, still on the lane. Something rattled under the bonnet for a second.

'Jesus. Looks like Greebo's still here, probably living in that caravan,' he said.

Alison will say she saw how watchful he'd become, and observed him as if from a distance, as if on a screen, because it was like she'd become invisible to him. It was, she'll say now, as if he was willing something to happen, or not happen and it didn't matter whether she was there or not. But she felt suddenly exhausted, a battery run out. She'll say she remembers licking her fingertip and running it under her eye, thinking perhaps her mascara might have run. For something to say, she said, 'Do I look okay to you?' But Guy seemed entranced, watchfully alert, his gaze fixed on the farm, or that's what she'll say she remembers.

'Guy,' she said. 'Am I okay?'

And he turned to look at her like he'd just come round from hypnosis, she'll say, but he said, 'Yeh. Yes. You look fine, yes.'

She remembers fetching her handbag out from the footwell, finding a lipstick, and putting some on. Not much, just a bit.

'Yeh, you look all right,' Guy said, but he was focusing on the farm again, not even looking at her.

She'll say now, she'll admit, that she wanted to take a photograph of it, this farm, this place, if that's what it was, a place. In fact, she reached for her phone, and, as if he knew what she was thinking, Guy said, 'Don't.' So she did not.

And it was as if she'd conjured up a situation. At least that's what Alison will say. It was as if she'd dreamed it. They both saw it, they must have: the door of the farm opened, and a woman appeared. Impossible, as it was, from that distance to guess her age. She could have been fourteen or forty. According to Alison, she was wearing jeans, hung low on her hips as if it was a fashion, wellington boots, a donkey jacket,

14

and she seemed to be carrying something – a bag, perhaps, a carrier bag – swinging it like it might be a bag, that is. Guy put the car into first gear as if he was a learner driver, seemed to murmur something, and drove slowly towards the farm, towards this woman. Her face came into focus, her expression, like a photograph developing. When she saw them, she slowed her movements, in fact, as the car stopped, she stopped. She suddenly didn't seem to move an inch, suddenly exhausted, as if her legs were, as if she was emerging from a day's work in a mine or a foundry, or on the land, perhaps. The jacket she was wearing had mud on the elbows, her hair was loose and very long, unbrushed, exactly the same rust-red as Guy's. But Alison will say something must have registered with Guy first, before it registered with her, that is, because he said, 'Don't say anything,' and he cut the engine.

It was just before she got out of the car, Alison will say, that she realised that what the woman was, in fact, holding, was not a carrier bag at all, it was a baby.

≋

She probably hadn't ever imagined a woman like that. At least, that's the impression Alison will give.

When she describes this time, the first time she saw this place here, she'll tell about the sky being stone grey with the very endings, or perhaps beginnings, of the red streaks of night, and she remembers there were ribbons of emptied-out cloud. There is a deeper dark here, for sure, and she'll tell how she felt it more than saw it. And she'll tell how there was a day-moon, a half-moon, wrong-looking. She makes it sound magical, almost, because against all that, she'll say it made her look unreal, this woman, this strange but strangely familiar-looking woman, especially since, behind her in the near distance, there were unexpected blue-green stained hills flowing across the westerly horizon that made it seem like an eerie, surreal European view. She'll say she remembers a smell lying heavy too. Not unpleasant to her, that smell, that lowish hum of foxes and ammonia and diesel and old rain and smoke. She liked it then, Alison did, perhaps not so much now. There is always that smell at that time of the year, though, of course, Alison didn't know that then. She'll tell about the view she had from the field on the other side, of the high-rises of Birmingham and the Black Country, and before that even, dim, distant, smudged-out outlines of the past-in-dustry of Smethwick, Tipton, Dudley, then Stourbridge – names of places Guy had only briefly mentioned to her. There were a couple of lambs, she remembers, that had been made sand-coloured by the earth there, and there was that caravan pitched up, old, papery looking, and sitting slightly out of true, ungainly, on bricks a little distance from the house itself. There were plastic hanging baskets each side of the door of the farm, discoloured – weathered, really – with thin grey strands of trailing ivy. She hadn't expected this, this patchwork quilt of a place, neither one thing nor the other. She can't say exactly what she'd been expecting. And, she'll say, getting out of the car, her head still heavy with suppressed migraine, the steepness of the hill behind her and the hawthorn and the bracken, and the dry-stone wall, she felt, something. What? What was it? Too hard for her to describe. And anyway, memory is an unreliable thing. Looking back almost always colours things differently. She'll say, though, that Guy walked on ahead of her.

'Donna,' he said, and the lambs sighed and scattered towards the top.

The woman – Donna – her face was slack, but her eyes were

wary. Alison could hear her breathing and will tell how she thought it was as if there was some issue going on with that, like she might have some sort of disfigurement or problem, or perhaps she was just simply worn out.

'Donna,' Guy said, again. And his voice was quiet and he was approaching her like you might approach a wild animal.

She said something, this Donna did, maybe, Guy's name. Something like that, and in hearing her speak, Alison recognised something in her, at least she'll say that now. She seemed to move through a series of different emotions, this woman, from fear through anger then sadness and then something else that Alison can't even name. Alison will say she watched as this woman, this Donna, seemed to try to lean in to kiss him. But Guy moved very slightly backwards and it was the air she kissed, the gap in between them. The sleeve of her jacket made her look like a giant moth or an injured bird. Alison will tell how she saw the baby held by its clothes, like an accessory in Donna's free hand, swinging, unbelievably against her thigh.

'Here,' Alison said, stepping forward. 'Let me, shall I just . . .'

She'll say she meant to take hold of the child, conscious of the cold wind, of the hardness of the cracked paving slabs, of the piles of mud or muck, of a bucket of murky-looking water just there, next to Donna's feet, conscious of a certain feeling having been sharpened within her, but Guy stepped back, put out his hand to stop her.

'Alison,' he said, and he said it like a warning. 'This is Our Donna. My sister.'

'*This* is Donna?' Alison said. She hadn't meant to say it like that. She'll say the air, the weight of the wind up there took her breath and made it sound like that. And so, to soften it, she'd said, 'Oh.' And her voice had carried, and Donna looked at her, looked through into her, so she'll say, and it was like a guard had come up all around the place.

Looking at her then, looking at this sister of his, Alison will say she saw the weird likeness between them, but all she'll mention now is the colouring, the flicker of red in the hair, perhaps the flash of something about the eyes.

No-one moved, not even the baby, who, when Alison looked, was awake, but was unnaturally quiet. Donna was holding it by its clothing at the chest, her knuckles white from the effort, her arm poker-straight down by her side. The baby's back was arched almost into a semi-circle, the limbs flaccid, limp. Alison will say she'd never seen a child, a baby, carried like that in her life. It made her feel a plunge like butterflies, like nerves, like guilt.

Alison will tell how she tried to smile, but she hadn't realised how frightening her smile might appear to a stranger until then. Guy took her by the arm. It was, she'll say, all so tentative.

'This is Alison,' Guy said.

The woman, Donna, seemed to relax. She moved her mouth but no sounds came. Guy said, 'Shall we . . . ?' and he motioned inside, and somehow, they all moved towards the farm. Alison was watching the child, the baby. She'll say the look of it, hanging there at the fingertips of this woman, suspended like a shopping bag, it was bizarre, but she'll tell how Guy stopped, just for a second outside the door, his feet planted, his posture somehow different, as if, she'll say, he was addressing the place, as if he was preparing to reattach himself to it. And as they walked through into the house, she'll say she noticed the door, the bottom panel was cracked, as if someone had tried to put their foot through it.

She has a particular memory of her first impressions of

the place. She'll say there was a certain kind of cool inside that first part of the house where boots and wellingtons were kept, odd bits of kindling in piles, and coats and hats hung up on a wall-mounted coat rack. She wiped her feet on the rush mat – the one that might have said 'Welcome' once – but no-one else did. She'll say she saw Guy shiver at the change in feel there. Good, she'll say she thought, I'm glad you felt that. I'm glad I wasn't the only one. The sound of the door, the swollen wood of it against the lino when he pushed it to, the lambs heard, and seemed to stop to watch the house, unperturbed by any of it. And the kitchen, it had this *smell*, to her, of dogs and spices and old cooking and mud and burnt things. It ought to have been embarrassing, that smell, straight away, she'll have thought.

It must have been that Donna, having led them into the kitchen, into the farm, put the baby down somewhere, into a crib, perhaps, because Alison will say she remembers Donna stretching her arms out, walking across to the Belfast sink, letting water run fast from the tap, filling a glass, and drinking. Alison will say how she watched her drink it, how a couple of old paper Christmas decorations hanging on a hook near the window flapped. She'll say Guy sat down at the table, and then Donna did, the glass of water in her hands. She'll say she could feel something like electricity coming off her, this woman, this Donna. That's how it seemed to her, just then. But she'd been up since six, and what with the travelling and her migraine issues and whatnot, she'd probably not felt quite herself.

What does she say she noticed? A vase of blown roses on the window sill; a 1950s cream-coloured Aga; a cat with a swollen belly sprawled on the worktop, licking its paw; dogs, black and white Border Collies, two of them, nosing through rubbish bags in the corner; an ancient-looking armchair (horsehair, she says she could definitely smell that); a baby's bottle half-full overturned on the table, dripping something brown like tea from the teat; a wooden clothes-horse draped with men's underwear; letters in brown envelopes roughly torn open and left on the worktop next to the sink.

An oversized old fridge clicked into life and buzzed loudly, next to it a washing basket, and a bucket of cloudy water similar to the one outside.

Guy said, 'How you doing, Donna?' And she seemed to shrug, said something Alison didn't hear, because of the noise from the fridge, but addressed, anyway, secretly to Guy. Alison will say she thought then how her accent, the Black Country accent that is, seemed designed to hint at defensiveness or perhaps sadness, the prospect of it. Guy got it, she could see that, he understood. He looked at her and shook his head as much as to say the dialect wouldn't survive translation anyway. He shoved a chair with his foot and motioned for her to sit. From outside, the lambs watched the three of them through the kitchen window. They'd have been able to see Alison sit down, and see her shoulders tense. They'd have been able to see Donna take a long drink from the glass, her eyes half-closed, her neck, long in the swallow of it. They'd have been able to see her place the glass down on the table, sit back in the seat as if getting comfortable, they'd have been able to see her weighing things up. Alison, though, will say she remembers how, sitting there, there was more than just a smell about this place, there was a proper *feel* of it that she hadn't expected. There was a stillness of air inside there that seemed to hold something primitive.

For something to say, she said, 'It's nice here. Peaceful.' And she was looking around, at the state of the Aga, at the dishes all haphazard in the sink.

Donna, she'll say, seemed to be sitting very still, as still as bones, stiller, even, and they were all quiet for a bit, except for the dogs who must have found something to eat in the bags, and there was the fluster of water in the drain, and the vibrating buzz from the fridge. Then Donna said, 'Have you told her?' And Guy swallowed hard and looked away, past her, past Alison. 'Have you?' she said, a little louder. 'Does her know, this woman, here?'

Alison will say she noticed how strangely *softly* she spoke, how little pressure she placed on each syllable. It should have been exhausting to listen to because there seemed no variation, no pull and push. But the inelegance of that was mesmerising. It was. Alison had been used to hearing the way Guy spoke, how every now and then, the way he periodically relaxed back into this odd mother-tongue. To her, the Black Country way of using words was one thing, but the tune they used, the strange rise and flatness, together, it often flummoxed her. Now though, Donna was different. It was like she was sleep-walking into the sentence in a moaning, whining way. She'll say she remembers how Donna took another drink from the glass, of how she closed her eyes and how it seemed like it was the sweetest thing.

Guy didn't answer. He looked like he was about to, but Alison will say a look came over his face as if there was something repulsive somewhere, and that look took her aback for a moment. She'll say, though, that she could definitely see the likeness between him and his sister just then.

She'll say she thought it was a rumble of thunder she heard, like an over-excited heart-beat, but when she looked, it was Flood – she knew it was him straight away – still tall despite the stoop, stepping into the room from the hallway, his hair foil-silver in that light, the sleeves of his shirt rolled up, his biceps flexing against the weight of carrying something in one hand, a cigarette in the other. Thin strands of grey on his arms and on the back of his neck and through the V of his open shirt were like life forms, and he stood, Flood did, his feet – his stockinged feet – like huge paws. She'll tell how he'd shuffled in, like there might be something going on with his hip or his foot.

'This woman?' Flood said, the words coming out in wisps of smoke. 'Am ya talking about a woman, Donna? Which woman's that, then? This one 'ere?' And he lifted his hand, and pointed, and it was trembling under the weight of what he was holding.

She spoke, Donna did, but Alison can't remember what it was she said. She'll admit though, that she noticed something about the way Donna seemed to put some sadness into Flood, into how he stood, how his chest rose and fell like that.

'Dad,' Guy said. And he stood up, faced his father. 'Shall we put that down?'

Alison will tell how the air in that kitchen seemed to become thick with something and she had to quickly adjust her mind. He, Flood, was exactly as she'd imagined he would be. Even the smell of him. Everything.

Flood had put the claw hammer down on the kitchen table, he had placed it there – because that was what he'd been holding, pointing at Alison – and he had stood up as straight as his back would allow, had stubbed out his cigarette on a saucer. They all, all of them, looked at it, the hammer there on the table, next to the baby's bottle. Nobody moved. The buttons on Flood's shirt strained, the hairs underneath there were bristling, the flesh underneath them was flushing red. Alison will say she saw the wildness in him then, she saw him as something more than human. And then he smiled at Guy,

22

or there was a baring of teeth, hard for Alison to tell which. Donna didn't say anything, but Alison will say she'd never seen anyone change or correct their expression like that before, so that close to, she, Donna, looked, according to Alison, suddenly older. She'll say there was a sense of the town about her, like there was the grime of industry etched into little lines round her eyes. Donna was thin, she could see that, and there was something breakable about her, but the way she was sitting, the way she looked then, at Flood, made everything feel charged up. As far as Alison was concerned, at that moment, Donna wasn't doing anything she could put her finger on, but sitting there, breathing the air in that kitchen, both feline and nervy at the same time, as if she held a knowledge of something that she thought – she hoped – no-one else knew anything about. But, see, Alison did know. She knew everything.

※

The sun shone bright and sudden through the window. Flood leaned across Alison so close she could smell his strange fiery sweetness. He was offering his hand to Guy, who seemed to hesitate and only briefly held the tips of his fingers. Alison will say she could feel a sort of compressed anger coming from both of them.

Flood said, 'Guido?' And then, without looking at her. 'This woman 'ere?'

'Alison, Ali,' Guy said, and then to her, 'My father.'

And she's sure she saw Guy wipe his hand on the back of his jeans.

Flood gazed at her then, his eyes, the irises, made piercing by a certain inner clouding. 'Ah, Ali,' he said. 'I thought you'd be a bloke.'

Donna let out a spluttered laugh, and then Flood did. Alison will tell how she glanced across at Guy, how there were blotches of red on his neck.

'Well,' Flood said. 'You did move down south.' And he lifted his hand, then let it drop, limp-wristed.

'It's the West Country,' Guy said. 'Actually.'

'*Actually*.' Flood's way of saying it, mirroring it, Alison will say, was terrifying. 'Same difference,' he said, and he pitched to the left a little before steadying himself and sitting down heavily on the armchair in the corner. A puff of grey dust squeaked out from somewhere towards the back. Alison will say it was like he was presiding over them all.

'Actually?' Donna said. She was aping Guy, and Alison will say she remembers clearly that she saw something empty out of him, Guy, for a split second.

There was a sound, a squeak, rodent-like, but Alison will say only she seemed to hear it.

'The West Country.' Flood said it under his breath. 'Like as if you wanted to get as far away from us as possible.'

And she'll say Guy took a deep breath, as if he was trying to erase, or suck in those words of his father's. He moved, really quickly, to the window, said, 'So, what's with the scaffolding then?'

And she'll tell how Flood was rolling a cigarette, making it look like an art form. Cross-eyed, she'll say he was, with concentration.

'Roof,' he said, and he started licking the cigarette paper. His tongue, she could see, was coated with something brownish. 'Or chimney, or summat.'

When he lit it, the cigarette, it flared a little and hissed as he sucked at it. The smoke came out in a fast, thin line from of the corner of his mouth.

24

'Bit of damp upstairs on the chimney breast in our Ivan's room. Leak. From the flashin' probably.'

At the sound of his brother's name, Guy hesitated a second. Again, there was that rodent cry. It was the baby that was making the noise. Not exactly a cry. More piercing than that. Alison will say the sound was going through her. She could see then that the child had been put into the washing basket, she could see the kick of a limb, like a spasm through the gaps in the plastic wickerwork.

'Who's doing it, the work up there?' Guy said.

'Who's doin' it?' Flood's voice rose an octave, his fingers twitched around the arms of the chair. 'Who d'ya thinks doin' it?'

Guy sighed. 'You don't want to be climbing up that scaffold, Dad. Get somebody to do it for you,' he said.

Flood rocked forward a couple of times, trying to get comfortable, probably. The ash was fluttering about and landing on the arm of the chair, Alison will say she remembers that.

'Who else can do it?' he said, his voice loud then, incredulous. 'Not our Ivan.'

Donna, Alison will say, stood up.

'No.' Guy was getting flustered and Alison could hear it. 'I mean, you know, pay somebody to sort it properly. Get some other stuff done as well.'

He was motioning around the room, his hand flapping like it was like a ballet move. Alison will say he had a point, the place was tired, the walls were stained - nicotine, she thought, grime - and the plaster was loose and missing in places, and that was just the kitchen.

'You know.' Guy was beginning to sound a bit defeated. 'Sort it all out, all this. Get Greebo to do it. He's still here, right?'

Donna had picked the baby up and was adjusting its position so that it lay upright against her shoulder, its face peering out through strands of her hair, its mouth a toothless pinkish hole, there was cigarette ash on its head. She was patting its back and the crying had developed into a series of coughs, according to Alison, and the sound was like a tree trunk being chopped. Donna brought the baby over to the table and stood next to Guy.

'No point now, anyway,' Flood said. 'Anyway, I got a funeral to pay for.' And Alison will say there was a dip in his voice she could almost feel sorry for, and he nipped off the lit end of his cigarette with his thumb and the ash fell, dying red, onto the lino.

'I'll pay for that,' Guy said, and then, turning to Alison. 'Won't we?'

The baby was squirming and nuzzling next to Donna's neck, but she was looking at Guy.

'What's his name? Or her?' Alison said. She was talking about the baby, she was mesmerised by it, but Donna seemed not to hear her.

'Oi,' Donna said. She was talking to Guy and he looked at her. Donna squinted at his face, and Alison will tell how she saw her concentrate, lift a crooked little finger and flick deftly that bit of grit out from the corner of his eye, and then wipe the tip of her finger across the baby's back.

'Him.' Flood was standing, seeming to straighten up in sections, or try to, his elbows pointing outward like wings, his hands, big with work and the cold, placed on his hips. 'It's a lad, the babby.'

'What's he called?' Alison said. 'What's his name?' She can't say why she thought it was important to know.

The baby was moving his head from side to side. Alison

will have been thinking how she'd seen big animals, lions, elephants on TV do something similar, swaying and weaving abnormally. She'll say she couldn't think what it was supposed to mean. He was grizzling, and she'll say she noticed that what he was wearing – the little vest or whatever it was – had a hole, singed like a cigarette burn at the back.

'Smiler,' Donna said. 'Ivan Smiler. That's his name, innit, Dad?'

Flood was straightening his back and it seemed to be making him growl. His eyes were flicking about the kitchen as if he was looking for something.

'Greebo won't do it,' he said. 'Heights. He don't like 'em. And anyway, there's no point now.'

Donna was plucking at the baby's cheeks. 'Tha's what I call him, anyway. He's alus smilin'.'

One of the dogs came over and started sniffing at Alison's jeans, licking the spot where she'd spilt the coffee. She had to shove it away.

'There's a letter here somewhere,' Flood said. 'Compulsory purchase.'

'What?' Guy said.

Donna pushed a brown envelope across the table.

'They want to knock the farm down to build the bypass,' Donna said.

The baby was making sucking noises. Donna was feeding him from the bottle. It looked like tea, definitely, Alison will say, or milk that wasn't quite fresh.

'Any road,' Flood said, 'we shall see about that.' His voice louder than it ought to have been. 'Our Ivan's through theer.' And he nodded towards the door.

'What?' Guy said. 'He's here?'

'Course he is,' Donna said.

'Open casket, in the front livin' room,' Flood said. He was rolling another cigarette, leaning against the fridge. 'Like your mother. Like me, if I could 'ave my way.'

Alison will tell how it was like Guy was holding his breath, only the baby's sucking and swallowing could be heard, how it seemed like a long moment, before Flood relit his cigarette, said, 'Well, am you gonna go through and see 'im, or not?'

⚡

Alison will tell that when Guy left the Black Country, he told her they all said he'd be back. You can't leave this behind, they said, this isn't so much a place, as part of your biology. They all thought it, and the fact of him being a twin, they all said would be another reason why he'd return. They thought he'd struggle, being separated, from Ivan, yes, but mainly his separation from the Black Country, people thought, would be the biggest problem for him. In some ways, they were right. But Alison knew exactly why he'd left, of course. He'd found himself by the sea, with different air and different people and an entirely different landscape, a different outlook. He'd put himself through a degree at university, had got himself a job with the local newspaper – that's where they'd met, him and Alison. He'd been different then. She'll say he was quieter, yes, thoughtful, odd, perhaps, a bit guarded. Looking back, she might say that at first there was a time when she thought she was beginning to understand him, where he was from, what the core of him was made of. He was a strange one to her, secretive, yes – but he was more complex than that – it was more like there was a sense of something, a seam of Black Country maybe that was running through him without mention, and

28

the way he talked about it, the farm, it was as if there was an unacknowledged magnetism of the place that filled him with such a deep sense of something like loss that he couldn't find words to explain it. This is what Alison will say. It had taken years for him to re-establish any sort of regular contact with his family. And though he eventually started phoning his Dad every Wednesday night, seven o'clock, the phone calls never lasted long. She'll say she eavesdropped, listened to the great periods of silence, wondered why he didn't talk about his job, about her. When Alison asked him why, she remembers very clearly how he just shrugged. But she knew why, of course. Of course, she did.

She'll say she listened to the way he spoke to his father on the phone, how he withheld information, how he made his life seem like much less than it was.

'But you'll be back,' Flood kept saying, which, Alison will say, is why he never went back, not even at Christmas or birthdays, not even when the farm had an outbreak of coccidiosis and a load of the lambs died. It had been nine years, going on ten, and he hadn't been back once, not even when they told him about Ivan being ill, not even when they put Ivan on the phone and his voice was that weak it didn't even sound like him – that was a year or so back.

'How are you, Ive?' she'd heard him say. 'How am you, mate?'

She'll tell how she heard him quietly lapsing back into a different voice, one she hadn't properly heard before.

She'll say she remembers it wasn't a long call, at least that's what she'll say now. And it was the last time he was to speak to Ivan. When he came off the phone, he said, 'He's just told me they're giving him Thalidomide. *Thalidomide.* Some sort of trial thing.' The words hung in the air like a pest. 'He's probably misunderstood.' He said it quietly. 'Thalidomide. Christ.'

He didn't go back to see Ivan, not even one last time. Alison might admit that she thought about trying to persuade him, but didn't. Their life was settled, the air was good – sea air – they both had good jobs, a nice flat, the beach wasn't far away. Guy said – no, he didn't *say*, this is something Alison probably just felt – he didn't want anything to change, so, obviously, nothing did. She'll say she made sure she kept things on an even keel, no matter what. *She* did that. Ask her now, and she'll say she thought Guy didn't much like change, that she tended to monitor his moods, the temperature of him. It was, given everything, she'll say, a brave thing for him to do, move away. Alison, anyway will say that. Perhaps, actually, it was braver for him to return.

෨

Guy could write a good article – an excellent one, in fact. He had a flair for facts and he could put information together in this water-tight way he had. He'd told Alison that and no-one knew where that came from. Nobody in his family had encouraged it in him – far from it. Guy would say how Flood would comment that, 'As our Ivan come out of the womb worrying, our Guy come out dreaming,' that writing was a 'nice hobby for girls'. Guy had told Alison that time and again Flood had said, 'But the farm's in your blood. It's proper graft, proper work.'

Guy left the farm on the day of his mother's funeral. Alison will say he told her that just as he was leaving, Flood had slapped him, hard, across his face, nearly knocked him off his feet. He'd written a note, Guy had, and had left it on the kitchen table, just a short one, not saying much except that he was going, but he'd got the timing all wrong and Flood caught him about to leave. He'd found it, the note, Flood had, and had reared up next to the door. Ivan had just walked in and must have caught the tail-end of this row, and when Flood slapped him, Guy would say he thought it was all about a show of strength, because he, Flood, needed to show Ivan something, some power, some authority. And he needed to warn him that folks don't just leave, and they don't leave this place. Flood had apparently shouted, of course, had told Guy he was a retard, an embarrassment, a fucking dunce, an underhanded bastard, that his mother, God rest her soul, would be ashamed. *Ashamed.* He'd told Guy he'd been nothing but a let-down, that his mother had cosseted him, spoilt him rotten, babied him. Flood had been drinking, naturally, everybody had, and Alison will say how Guy told her the smell of beer on his dad's breath was that fresh, it was like wet wood, like something grown from the earth there – that's how he'd described it to her. He told Alison he felt sorry for Ivan, leaving him there with Flood all riled up, spit flying out of his mouth, actual froth gathering in the corners like he was some kind of pit horse.

When he left, though, Guy took nothing with him except his savings, which wasn't much, so that made him feel right-eous, he told Alison. That he would have to make his own way, no matter what, seemed quixotic, bold. This is what Alison will say she thought at the time. He'd told her he'd hitched a lift in the first lorry that stopped. It was heading down the M5, southbound. Some delivery of stock to Plymouth. He'd never been further than Worcester before. He'd told her he'd slept rough at first, on benches and on beaches, he'd had to. By the time she met him, she'll tell how he looked like a vagrant, still, a proper wanderer, even though he'd been to university by that time and had sorted himself out with a bedsit in the city centre. He'd told Alison that Flood didn't, wouldn't, speak to him after he'd left like that. Refused to. When she and Guy had talked, and they had, about what they both wanted, like couples do, he'd been clear about how he felt about starting a family – or not, absolutely not. No children, he'd said, he was clear on that. And she'd imagined, only imagined, that was because of Flood, because he perhaps saw history repeating itself. And she went along with that. He'd been promoted at the newspaper. Editor now. And all the articles were left to the reporters, like her. Guy made the decisions.

What did she see in him? She'll say he was different. Quiet, a bit faraway, especially for the last year or so. He went for walks by himself. And she'll admit that she found herself monitoring him, watching him. It was, she says, as if there was a return to the first principles of their arrangement together, their relationship, that is. They're secretive, both of them, Alison and Guy. She's bad as him. She'll say she'd always felt there was something he wasn't telling her, that if she was patient, if she listened, he'd tell her. Perhaps now she knows, she wishes she hadn't been told.

And now they were back, here, in his Black Country.

⁂

Looking back, she'll say the pills she'd taken for her migraine were probably just about starting to work but she'll admit she felt so tired, as if in the midst of a dream, her vision still hampered by gentle tremors. She'll say she felt like she was looking at them, this family of Guy's, as if she was seeing them through a screen, from the inside of it out, as if she was seeing them like they were virtual things, as if she or they were floating about without point. Perhaps it was that, she'll say now, that made her imagine it all as they walked out of the kitchen, down the hallway. Flood led the way through, his limp more pronounced from the back. She'll say she remembers Guy hesitating, seeming to take a breath, seeming to straighten, to prepare himself, she'd thought at the time, and he'd followed Flood, trailing his hand for her to hold. To Alison, the hallway from the kitchen was long, thin, the door frames crooked, skirting boards greyed with dust. A door at the end was half-open, and they walked through. The 'front living room', Flood had called it, which was ironic. Someone had lit a fire in the cast iron hearth, and she'll tell how she could smell it, the fire, before she could see it or feel it. The logs must have been damp, and they seemed to sing, or scream, on top of the flames like tortured gremlins. Rather than heat, she'll say, the fire in the hearth was creating a draught and she'll say it was the smell of silage, of nature, from somewhere, wafting through, of muddy earth and wetted stone, and smeared antiseptic that she remembers most vividly. The curtains were drawn closed but for a narrow gap in the middle. A thin slice of light spangled through onto the far wall. But everything clashed: midnight blue walls, tangerine ceiling and blood coloured carpet. 'Jesus,' Guy said, but under his breath, she'll say she heard that.

There were a couple of lamps, dim-bulbed, daffodils – plastic – dusty, in a pottery vase, and there were ornaments of women and children, dressed in Victorian clothes, selling flowers or picking them. The metal frames of three photographs glinted on a low, wide sideboard: the twins, young, wearing school uniform, ungainly, chubby in the face, not quite smiling, identical except that one of them was blinking when the flash went off – she'll say now that she imagined it was Guy but can't say why; one of Flood and, she imagined, Paulette, Guy's mother, young, on their wedding day, and one of Paulette, wearing dark lipstick, a professional photograph, taken in a studio by the look of it, with her seeming to look at, or for, something far away. Alison will say now that she wanted to take a closer look at those photos, but Flood seemed to be standing guard. Still, she could see, even from where she was, that Guy had inherited not just his eyes from his mother, but a certain kind of expression, a certain way of positioning his chin, and she shivered, Alison did, and almost, but not quite, said, 'Feels like someone walking over my grave.'

Alison will say she assumed it was Flood who'd done it, lit the fire, that is, to take the chill off. She'd assumed it was his job to do that. She'd never lit a fire in her life. She didn't think, just then, that she knew how to, and she'll tell how she looked at the flames trying take hold of the wood and thought about how hopeless that looked, how large the logs were, how the flames struggled, and she will have been mesmerised by it. Her stomach was empty, except for the painkillers. It growled, an animal. Guy squeezed her hand, she'll say she remembers that clearly. And in shadow, against the wall furthest away was a cabinet. The glass, even in that light, she could see was dusty, but inside there was a shotgun, placed vertically, as if in a presentation box, and next to it a faded picture of Jesus, sagging on the cross, and beneath that, on a tall table, a light wood coffin.

She'll say she didn't know what they were expected to do. She'll have felt nervous, full of something she didn't know how to explain. She perhaps thought about leaving them to it, this was Guy's twin brother, after all, and she'd never even met him. She would have wondered if she could bow out, leave diplomatically, but when she turned to look for an escape route, Flood was standing in the doorway, a giant, on guard. She'll say she didn't know it was him straight away - everything is abstract in the dark, and it was dark to her then - and she'd perhaps felt exposed or a sudden sense of claustrophobia. It must have been odd, that situation she was in then. We might almost begin to feel sorry for her, perhaps. And she'll say he eyed her like the total stranger she was, Flood did.

'I was just,' she said, or started to say, to whisper, and her stomach gurgled, or the damp logs did, and she'll say she felt a peculiar type of heat creeping up from her feet and it made her feel faint. He didn't help her, Flood didn't. He didn't play his part in the conversation. He stood, his head tilted to one side, his whole frame, the whole of him, blocking the door, so she'll say. We might imagine that if they'd been actors with roles to play, it would have been like he'd forgotten his lines. So, she apparently said, 'I was just going to let . . .' and he seemed to take a breath, and she might have imagined she heard his bones creak. Donna sat down on the sofa there, the baby was wriggling and she placed it, him, she placed *him* face-down on her lap. Alison will say she remembers that.

'Wind,' Donna said, and Alison will tell how she was patting the baby's back like a drum.

And then, according to Alison, Guy stepped forward, and she followed him. And she'll tell how suddenly she saw the tip of a nose in the coffin, and the beginnings of a profile she couldn't help but recognise. Behind her, Flood was saying, "ere.' And when she looked, he was holding a beer bottle, and he held it up so she could see it, or Donna could. 'Give 'im a glass o' this,' he said, meaning the baby, or Alison remembers it that way.

There was an armchair, overstuffed, and Alison will say her

heel caught on one of the legs, and she stumbled and had to catch herself from flopping down onto it. One of the cats - a black one, a big one - she hadn't realised had been curled up on a cushion there, and it jumped and scurried out of the door and up the stairs. Guy was squeezing her hand, she'll say she could feel her knuckles grinding, and his, and for a moment, they were locked like that, Guy and her, as if they were one person. She loved it when he was like this. She won't say that, but it's a fact. She'll tell how she wanted to say something. She wanted to say, 'You all right?' and she wanted him to say, 'Yeh. You?' But nobody said anything, and somehow, it was like they were walking towards a fate.

Of course, she'll say she was nervous, never having seen a dead body before. And what she'll say she remembers is the whiteness of the silk, or satin, or whatever the material was in the coffin itself, she'll say she remembers the glint of the hinges, the way there was a glow, dim as a pilot light, across the wood; the body, the way the legs were, the feet - she'll have been able to see they'd tied the shoe laces together; the clasped hands, the nubs of fingertips so very white, the hangnail on the thumb, the rosary beads wound round, the sharp ironed crease in the trousers, the brown belt, slightly worn at the buckle, the collar and tie - a big knot. And the face, a strange mirror of Guy's. She'll say she'd seen Guy - perhaps she'd watched him - asleep like this, absent of sound and movement. But she'll say she remembers the way Ivan's flesh was creased at the neck, the ripple of skin there, the workings underneath imaginable, his Adam's apple, a large immobile stone in his neck. And the smoothness of the chin, shaved, ruddy, like a Sunday roast, and of it all being so still, very still, of course, yes, but supernaturally so, as if they - as if she - were in the presence of something absolutely unbelievable. She'll say she

36

remembers thinking, of the face, of Ivan's face, that it was, in face, just a slightly iller, older-looking mask of Guy's. It was – and she'll say this – a fact carved out of stone, like a saint or something. And what surprised her: the ear, a perfect little labyrinth, a puckered piercing – a *piercing* – in the lobe. A little mark of rebellion. She'll say it was instinctive when she touched her own ear, her own earring and briefly remembered the thrill of getting a piercing years ago, of the pain, and of how alive she felt, how individual.

Behind her, she'll tell how she could hear the baby sucking, and the sound of someone sitting down heavily and she felt tempted to turn and look because she didn't want to stare at the face there, at Ivan. She'll say she didn't want to. She looked at Guy instead, watched him breathing because she knew she could, because she knew he wasn't looking at her. She'll admit that she thinks she might have imagined it now, but to her then, there was a smell of cleaning fluid, and she was thinking how odd it was, how very odd it all was. But she'll say she could see it then, this unbroken thread between the two of them, these brothers, these twins. She could see it in Guy's face, and in the way he stood, the way he was holding himself, in the way he stared at Ivan like he might have been listening. There were shadows under Guy's eyes, a dull, steel blue, and, she'll say, he let go of her hand and touched – moved – a scrap of hair behind Ivan's ear, and a tiny piece of grit from somewhere near his eye. She'll say she felt herself recoil from the sight of that. But she looked at his face, then, Ivan's. She looked so closely – she made herself – and she could make out the individual eyelashes, the shape of his eyebrows, flecked, in the exact same way as Guy's, with gold. She'll say she could see scar tissue, little scars, above his cheek bone and a longer one above his eye that looked like it might have been stitched at one time. A life-time – a short one – in a face, she was thinking. And – what is it that makes people do this? – she'll say she felt like grabbing him, Ivan, by the shoulders. She'll say she felt like howling, or trying to resuscitate him with a primal scream or something. She might have imagined doing that would make his eyelids flicker and open, that he would take a deep breath and sit up. She might have imagined him smiling like Guy could smile. All a big joke. Not really dead. Haha. But, of course, she only imagined doing this, and thinking back about it now she'll say makes her feel like laughing. Laughing and shouting. Nerves or something. Because it isn't – wasn't – funny at all.

'A drink?' Flood said. It made her jump, and Guy, both of them.

'I mek it meself.' Flood was pouring brown liquid from a large bottle into half-pint glasses. 'I calls it "wine", but . . .'

He handed Guy a glass first, then her, and she watched as Flood poured some for himself into a large-handled glass.

'This is my glass, this,' he said, holding it up. 'Had it for years. Proper Stuart Crystal glass, this. Got me name etched on it, see?'

She could see something was inscribed along the top, and there was a pattern of precise cuts all the way round, the light was making it give out a rainbow prism effect. Flood flicked the rim with his thumbnail and it sent out a clear, high note. He smiled, said, 'Crystal, this. See.' And he flicked it again and the sound was extraordinary. 'Had it years.'

Alison will say she watched as he took two gulps of his drink, three. His neck, she'd have seen, was thick, and the skin there was like ill-fitting leather, as if there'd been, at some point in the past, some emptying out of something from the inside.

'Go on,' he said, pointing with the glass in his hand. 'Cheers, like. To our Ivan.' Maybe Donna shuffled in her seat or the baby did.

It was cloudy, the liquid in the glass, like apple juice is, or urine. It looked to her thick, gel-like. She'll tell how she sniffed at it.

'Go on,' he said. 'Cheers.' And he took another mouthful and she heard the effort of his swallow. Guy was looking into his glass as if it was a crystal ball. She'll say now that she'd never seen him drink alcohol in the whole time she'd known him.

'Go *on*,' Flood said, again. So, she'll tell how she let it wet her lips, as if she'd been issued with a dare to drink it. It was strong, the liquid. Yeasty. Still-fermenting-sour, not quite ready to drink yet. Flood's eyes, she remembered, brightened. She remembers him baring his teeth at her. Big teeth, yellow-ish but not crooked. To please him, to fit in, she says, she took a proper mouthful of it.

'Nice,' he'd said – perhaps it was a question – and she'll say she nodded, but automatically. She must have felt it go right down into her stomach, and settle there like river-water, on top of the painkillers.

'I haven't eaten much,' she said. 'So . . .' And she'll explain how she put the glass down on the arm of the chair.

'It ain't that strong,' he said, and he finished his drink and poured himself another. 'Sit down, why do'n you?'

It was, she'll say now, as if there was no-one else in the room, except her and Flood, or, better, as if the others were there, but in shallow-focus, and behind her, she'll say how she felt the photographs watching her.

'Is that Paulette?' she said. 'In those photos there.'

Flood looked, for a second, a bit lost. Alison will say he

looked like he thought she was trying to catch him out. She perhaps sensed, rather than saw something shift in the room. Looking back now, she'll say that Flood seemed to glance around, settle his gaze downwards, at the rug by the fire. So, she said, 'She looks really nice. Really pretty.' And then, 'They're lovely photos.' But it was for something to say and she'll tell how he seemed to flinch and filled his mouth with that wine of his, swallowed like it was painful, and inhaled sharply through his teeth.

'So, then,' she said, buoyed up, probably, by a sudden sense of confidence. 'Will there be any flowers?'

There was a sound of hiccups from somewhere, the baby most likely.

'Flowers?' Flood said.

'Yes,' she said. 'You know, for . . .' She meant for the funeral, or for Ivan.

Flood put his empty glass down on the arm of the sofa. Light from somewhere, the fire or somewhere, channelled through it onto the wall.

'I can't abear flowers,' he said. 'Lilies make me sick. I can't breathe for the stink of 'em.'

The logs were greyish, cooling in the fireplace, they'd never really taken, and she'll say he seemed to notice it and shivered, and that made her shiver, too. She'll say she remembers this, clear as day.

'Bloody fire,' he said, and he started poking at the logs with an old walking stick that had been kept by the side there, near the hearth. What light was thrown out seemed to settle in stains on the rug.

Alison will say she watched him doing this, saw how slowly he moved, more deliberately than she'd have expected. When she glanced towards the doorway, there was a light on in the kitchen, she remembers she could see it casting out along the worn carpet on the hallway floor. Flood was stooped down next to the hearth, his profile seemed, to her, all nose, and she'll say she thought at first that he might have been trying to re-light the fire using some kind of psychic ability. Of course, she would have just started to feel that drink working inside her, there was already that light-headedness, what with the painkillers and so on. Perhaps it was that. But she'll describe how she watched Flood, there by the hearth. Maybe she watched him like you or I might watch a TV programme, or a play. She'll tell how she watched him pick up a sheet of newspaper, fold it into some origami-shaped thing and place it in amongst the logs. She watched his big fingers, and his swollen knuckles. Working hands. She watched as he struck a match against his own palm, and lit the paper. She watched as he used the same match to light a thin cigarette he'd picked up from the mantel-shelf. He was, she might say, the master of that fire as the logs started to yield to the flames. When he stood up, it was as if he'd completely forgotten she was there, or any of them were.

'Her 'eart was a bit too close to the surface,' Flood said.

Alison will say she watched his face shivering with light from the flames.

He straightened, as best he could, and turned. 'Paulette, I'm on about. I keep tellin' our Donna that, not keepin' 'er 'eart where anybody can see it.'

He took a long drag from his cigarette, glanced over at the photographs. 'That never does here, in this place, bein' like that, bein' saft. You 'ave to learn to be 'ardened.'

Alison will say she thought Flood seemed to look through her, and she felt the air between them tighten.

'Cheers,' she said, and she picked up her glass and took a

long drink, and it was like a display of obedience, perhaps to harden herself.

Flood, watchful of her, did not move a muscle.

A log cracked like a gunshot in the fireplace, but no-one jumped, not even the baby, and everybody seemed, to her, to come back into focus.

Guy, she'll say, seemed to appear, seemed to materialise, as people do in dreams, and he brushed past her, and she swears she felt an electric shock along her arm.

'Hadn't we better start getting ready?' he said. 'Car's'll be here soon, won't they?'

And perhaps it was the fact that the fire was so noisy, revving up, roaring within a minute, that no-one seemed to hear Greebo, a short man in oversized overalls, his greasy hair in a pony tail, come into the room.

'Oh,' he said, when he saw her, or maybe Guy. It was like he'd seen an apparition. 'I thought . . .'

Flood jerked his head, his jaw set, his back straightened. Everyone surely heard it click, his back, so Alison will say.

'Cars?' he said. 'What cars you on about?'

Greebo sat down next to Donna, put his arm round her shoulders, but kept his eyes on Guy, fascinated, it seemed. The baby wriggled on Donna's lap, an insect caught in a trap.

'Funeral cars,' Guy said. 'You know . . . or just the one car. I mean, I can drive me and Alison in mine.' And she'll say she remembers how he seemed to look at her as if he needed her to back him up, and she'll say his face, just then, the skin of it, sagged and she didn't want to, but she thought about Ivan's face.

Flood scratched his neck and a raspy mark bloomed instantly, and tiny flakes of skin floated about, caught in the beam of light through the gap in the curtains. It made Alison shudder automatically. She'd have felt like she couldn't move from Guy's side and held her breath, afraid she'd breathe in something other than air. Greebo stared at her and Donna shifted in her seat. The baby lay still on her lap.

༜

They'd got the date wrong – he had, that is. Guy. He'd thought Ivan's funeral was planned for the day they arrived, the afternoon. Actually, he'd got it wrong. The funeral was the next day. He told Alison he was sure, *sure*, that they'd said 15th, not 16th. Alison will say she remembers how Donna had looked at him like he'd lost his mind when he'd asked when people were going to get changed and ready, when the car was due to come. 'Termorrer,' she'd said. And he'd looked like his heart had fluttered and contracted, according to Alison. He'd offered to find a hotel – The Talbot would have some rooms, it always does – but Flood was adamant. 'Don' be so saft,' he said. 'Don' get spending your money. Your room's here. Our Donna'll sort it.'

And here's what Alison will say she remembers: walking down that narrow hallway, touching Guy on the arm, asking – whispering – if he was okay, how he felt about seeing his brother lying there like that, his identical twin brother. And how Guy flinched, gritted his teeth, angry, said, 'How d'you think I feel?' And how he walked on ahead of her, how his countenance changed. She'll say that in the kitchen, a cat was vomiting on the lino, one of the dogs was eyeing it happening. They'd all walked through from the front living room, and to Alison, it looked like a low-budget film set in that kitchen.

'You two can sleep in your old room,' Flood said. 'Donna, mek the bed up.'

43

Flood blew his nose on a big yellowing handkerchief, and, just for a second, he looked at the contents. Donna had the baby against her chest, and when it moved – when *he* moved – there was an imprint of her cardigan, like a brass rubbing on his cheek. It had rained while they'd been in the front living room, and the air in the kitchen was thick with damp. There was a smell of sourness and wet cigarette ends.

'I'll give you a hand.' Alison said it to Donna because she needed something to do and couldn't take her eyes off what was going on with the cat.

'S'all right,' Donna said, absent-mindedly, or so it seemed.

'Well, do you want me to . . .' Alison will say she held out her arms, and the baby looked at her with a strange indignance, like she was an enemy. That's how it felt to her. Donna and Greebo moved back slightly, together. Alison will explain it as if it was like a dance move, peculiarly balletic.

'Her's OK,' Flood said. 'Leave her be.' His tone was quiet but his shape, according to Alison, seemed suddenly both human and animal, intermingled. Donna seemed to understand this code and, without speaking, stood, slung the baby up against her chest, and appeared to drift off, out of the kitchen.

Flood sat, and Guy did, and Alison will say she remembers hearing the creak of floorboards in the room above, and tried to imagine the stripping of a bed, and the unfolding of sheets. She'll say Greebo stood watching them all and she saw him move his lips as if he was reciting something to himself. Something was rattling – a kettle, she realised – on the Aga. 'Shall I make us some tea?' she said, because she'll have needed to be *doing* something, she'll have wanted to connect herself in some way. But she'll say all three men remained stock-still, neither one of them seeming sure of the next move. She'll tell that she felt like she'd been placed into a situation, transplanted there from reality, into this strange, quiet, other rhythm. She might even tell how she was asking herself: what should I be doing? What should I be doing, exactly?

'Shall I?' She said it to Guy. She meant to ask if she should go and help Donna, but there seemed, to her, to be a telepathy going on between them, these men, and she was bewildered by that, so she'll say. Guy, she'll say, looked at her as if he suddenly didn't really know her. Anyway, she remembers having a splitting headache by that time, and there was the cat, and the dogs there still watching, and the smell, this *smell* of them all, all of it, in there, which was making her feel sick. What she most likely wanted to do was lie down, just for a couple of hours, or better, go home. And she was thirsty, and the glass Donna had left on the table was empty. She'll tell how she picked it up, not brave enough to ask for water.

'That last ewe'll need tending to,' Flood said, and his chair groaned as he leaned back. And upstairs, the patter of footprints, the sound of the baby whimpering was, Alison will say, deafening to her.

The cat, the one that had been sick, quite suddenly dashed out and one of the dogs followed it. Alison will tell how she noticed how pregnant it was, that cat, just then. Greebo had to move to one side.

Guy stood up and everyone looked. She'll say she remembers this.

'Do you need a hand with anything?' he said.

Greebo shook his head, but she remembers how it took him a second or two, and how he glanced - it was just a micro-second, really - at Flood, and she'll say she's sure she saw something about Guy's face, the eye, twitch. It was a long few seconds later, and Guy said, 'Right then, I'll just

. . .' And they all watched as he walked past Greebo, and out, down the hallway. It was as if he was following the cat, with his head down like that, the way he moved. They all heard he had to pull the door to a couple of times before it would shut after him.

In the kitchen, Flood had said, 'Gone to get your bags, I suppose.' He was talking about Guy, it was like he was explaining, and he was gazing out of the window. Greebo, though, had stood watching her like she was some kind of other being, more than a stranger, an enemy, an incomer. She'll tell how there were little things floating in front of her eyes like gnats might, and her head was pounding. The smell of what the cat had left behind was making it worse, and is something that will always, she'll say, remind her of this day.

When Donna came down, she was without the child. There were milk stains on her cardigan. What it was about her, and how she made Alison want to be something to her, is hard to explain.

'It's ready then,' she'd said, Donna had, and Flood stood up, as if in sections, and he motioned towards the door, and Alison followed him upstairs.

She'll say the carpet up there was the thinnest she'd seen, every footstep seemed heavy, and the landing was long, or longer than she'd imagined it to be, with doors off it like a strange hotel.

Flood was in front of her, walking in his odd, limping way. She'll say she remembers him saying, 'That's me son's room, that one,' and jerking his head sideways. 'And this is Guy's just 'ere, like.' He stopped then, outside a door, and let his voice go quiet and she must have wondered if he was embarrassed by what he'd just said.

There was a latch on the door, it made that loose metal

46

chink of a noise. You had to use your thumb to click it open. It hadn't been painted for a good while, the door, and where it ought to have been white, it was yellowish and peeling.

'In 'ere,' Flood said as he opened that door, and Alison will say how he quickly looked in, and she did, at the slope of the wall, the crocheted bedspread, the cheap set of drawers and wardrobe, and the view out. And he'd said, 'This'd be it. Him out there used to 'ave it.' He'd meant Guy, of course. 'Before he went and left.'

When she walked in she'll say she saw that the glass pane of the window was cracked in the corner and there was condensation and pooled water on the sills. She could see her breath. Outside, there were rainclouds forming, she could see, and hopeful birds clustered on branches of trees made to look diseased by the light. She must have been able to see almost as far as Birmingham from where she stood. She'll tell how there were lights down in a dip, strange, like a bowl of glitter. Car headlights, she'll have thought, leading to where, she didn't yet know. She'll tell how the air in that room seemed to be developing like some kind of chemical reaction. She'll say she remembers this though: Flood, when she turned round, had gone, leaving the door unlatched, part-open, and when she sat on the bed, she'll have heard the springs of it creaking.

She'll say it was strange, sitting there on Guy's bed and imagining him as a boy there, or a younger man. There were bits of old, brown Sellotape on the wall behind the bed. She picked a piece off, and it took a bit of the woodchip wallpaper with it. She'll say she imagined pictures of footballers, or women, pulled out from magazines. In the corner, dusty cobwebs swayed like the rigging of a ship and there was a dark stain on the ceiling above the bed. There were two short shelves, glossed in white paint, empty and in need of dusting, and on the wall, there was a laminated sheet which, when she looked closely, was complicatedly hand-drawn, a black and white mish-mash, with the title 'Map of the Black Country by Guy Flood.' The wardrobe, when she opened it, was also empty but for a couple of wire hangers and a smell of mould. It was, she'll say, a deserted room, a room cleared out, a dead man's room. There was a wooden chair, and an old electric heater next to the door, and she moved it closer to the bed. The flex wasn't long enough to be too close, and when she flicked it on, it warmed to life slowly and she'll describe how she could smell the burning dust. She'll say she lay down on that single bed – and she liked that, a single bed, the thought of it – but only for a minute. She'll tell how she ran the back of her hand over the woodchip wallpaper on the partition wall and thought about how Guy might have done the exact same thing years ago. She'll say she tried the switch on the bedside lamp, but the bulb had gone, or something, and the light in there seemed to be failing as if it was later than it really was, and she needed to take more painkillers. She'll say she intended to go to the bathroom, to run some cold water, take a couple of paracetamol, have a rest. But the landing, when she went out onto it, seemed like an Ames room. All perspective seemed, to her, to be skewed. There seemed too many doors, all closed, or as good as. Alison will say she looked at the door next to Guy's room. Flood had said, 'That's me son's room.' And, of course, the more Alison thought about him saying that, the more curious she became.

It had been Ivan's room. And the door was closed, but she'll say she remembers how it opened absolutely silently, and she remembers the smell of sour carpets and antiseptic in there. And what did she see? An actual dead man's room: a black cast-iron fireplace with a half-burnt log, greyish; a round paper lampshade hanging from the ceiling, torn a bit at the bottom, slightly askew; a wall painted emerald green at the head of the bed. Red everywhere else. Everywhere, except the ceiling, which was littered with luminous stars, various sizes, stuck on. On one of the bedside tables there were tissues, an empty glass clouded with finger marks, a plastic beaker you might give to a toddler and a soft porn magazine. There was a comb, which Alison picked up and held for a while because it had sprigs of hair tangled in it, the same colour as Guy's, that reddish colour. The double bed had a drip-stand next to it and had been badly made with the candlewick bedspread thrown carelessly over it. There was a sense of someone's head having lain on the pillow fairly recently. She'll say she thought if she were to touch it, the pillow, it might have still been warm, perhaps. There was an old walnut dressing table, and a desk, and on it, a candle, matches, a notebook and a jam jar, containing a couple of blunt-ended pencils and a biro. There was a plastic chair, grey, like one you might see in a secondary school, and she sat on it and felt it flex. She'll tell how she sniffed the candle – something slightly woody, incense, maybe, half burnt. There was a wheelchair, folded, next to the wall, and crutches. There were boots, unpolished, next to a wardrobe, and there was a carrier bag which, when she looked, was full of little brown pill bottles, plastic containers and small sachets. In the corner, there was a small yellow bin with 'Sharps' printed on it in red. Someone had put a couple of hot water bottles on top of it. Above that, two short wooden shelves, attached to the wall with grey metal hinges, and on which there were three or four paperbacks. Under her feet there was absolutely no give in the carpet when she walked over to have a look. The shelves were slightly out of line, or the ceiling was, so the whole effect was strangely demonic. She'll tell how she had to look closely at the spines of the books. And one of them was *God's Country* by Guido Flood. She'll say she had to read the title twice, three times, and the name: Guido Flood. Guy. She'll say she didn't know Guy had written a novel. Perhaps she didn't. She'll tell how she lifted it off the shelf, and she'll say something about how it made her feel a sort of confused sentimentality and pride. Which might be true. But really, she was angry, though she'll never admit it, she'll never actually say that. The cover was black with the title in yellowish blocked font. There was no picture. When she opened it, the spine cracked as if it was tight, new, not well put together, unread, self-published, and she was sure she could smell the ink on the pages. And there was a handwritten inscription: 'To I from G. Absolution,' it said. And she'll admit it was then that she felt a horrible jab of something. Not confusion. She'll tell how she flicked the pages and felt the air it made against her face. It opened at the first chapter. She'll say she read only the first line: '*Can you imagine your whole life being about the worst thing you ever did?*' She might have stayed in there longer. She could have read on a bit – she doesn't say this, but she probably would have. But, make no mistake now, she'll say that this, all this – the book, she means – was a surprise to her. And she'll say it as if it explains everything.

She's evasive, of course. She'll talk about how she heard voices downstairs. She'll say she thought Guy might be back with the bags. She'll say she left the novel on the desk there as she hurried out, onto the landing. Just left it there, unread. She'll say she was more concerned about the baby, she just wondered where the baby was, which room, and why he – why everything – was so quiet here, and then she'll say she heard voices, rising into an argument, Flood saying something, then shouting it. 'Nobody 'asn't asked you,' he said, and his voice thundered up through the ceiling and she heard the terrible sound of wood scraping against the lino. Donna answered, she'll say, though she couldn't hear exactly what was said. She'll explain about Flood, and how he was not giving up. She'll say she imagined him walking the length of the kitchen, that a chair had been upturned, and that Donna might be the one to set it right. She imagined one of the dogs being watchfully alert in the corner there, of a cat sliding itself between the Aga and the fridge. She only imagined this, of course. She'll have heard Flood cough, and might have been sure there was the striking of a match, positive she could smell the first breath of cigarette smoke, and Flood saying, 'There'll be hell to pay.' She's sure of that, so she'll say.

See. She's evasive. She thinks she can change the subject and you – we – will just take a different path, that she can change the rhythm of things just like that. She's slippery. Make no mistake about that.

⁂

Alison will insist she didn't know the whole story, or didn't think she did. Ask her, and this is what she'll say. She's adamant. Guy only told her what he wanted her to know, is the way she puts it. There were always gaps. Perhaps there were. But she had, of course, wondered about this place he was from. She'll say that sometimes he would talk about it in such a way that she'd thought he wanted to return. Now she was here, now she'd seen him here, she'll say she could see how it was as if he'd grown from the soil here, all sand and grit. She'll say something about how she observed him, like a bystander. She'll say she realised though, how he was now oddly out of place here now, how he seemed unable to let himself fully exist in this place. And she wondered, she'll say, how much of what he'd told her was accurate. How much of it could be, that is. Everything here seemed, to her, so anciently fixed, it was easy to think nothing had ever changed here, or ever would, but she'll say there was a sense that the paths were rearranging themselves and that, surely, this was not his life here any more, not even his past life. It was someone else's - a friend's life, or a friend of a friend's. This is what she'll say. What did she think was happening? Some kind of erasure? To her, it seems to make perfect sense. Guy wasn't exactly *her* Guy here. She didn't recognise him. To her, at least, this is what she will say it was like. But she is, of course, obsessed with secrets, Alison is, which is why all this, all this story here, the truth of it, is so difficult for her. Still.

She'd taken a nap that first afternoon, had fallen asleep on Guy's bed. It had been a long journey, in every sense, to this place after all, and her migraine was in a different stage, the stage that makes dreaming and migraines seem able to co-exist. She'll tell how she dreamed vividly about red slatted light from the gap in the curtains, how she imagined it had made patterns on the skin of her arm like little moving maps or live tattoos. She was sure she could hear voices like flushes of sound from downstairs, and imagined, in that curious state of amazement that isn't quite of this consciousness, that there was already soft, sliding strata beneath her, making up a new lay of the land. She'll say she heard or felt the sound of water from nearby, and there was a sense of home to her, but that was different here, and, anyway, in this dream, Guy was beside her, awake, still dressed, and it was as if she'd wished him there.

She'll say, in this dream, she moved to kiss him, but he seemed to sense it and shifted away.

'I didn't realise you were Catholic,' she heard herself say to him. This, though, was not true. His body, she remembers, was perfectly still, his profile, it struck her then, was exactly the same as Ivan's.

'Lapsed,' he said. 'Obviously.'

She'll tell how, in this dream, she could stretch and pull the curtain open a bit. Sitting up, she could see that clouds had formed into something weighing heavy, as if it was getting on for nightfall or morning, if she strained, she could see tower blocks in the far distance, and the spire of a church and a couple of tall chimneys and white smoke and some dreamlike, imaginary border between town and country. She'll say she was sure she could hear the sound of metal – a train rattling along a track perhaps like a deep, rhythmic, painful hum. She'll say she felt struck by some kind of remnant of her migraine about then, a dull, featureless pain with no real integrity. She'll say something about reaching for Guy's wrist to try and see his watch.

'It's only half two,' he said, and his voice seemed thick and lazy, not his, really.

It was cold, and she shivered. 'It's a bit weird having him here,' she said. 'You know, the body of him.'

She lay back down, against Guy, for the warmth. It was a single bed, remember, and Guy lifted his arm then so that she could get closer. She put her head on his chest and will say she felt him yield to her. His skin smelled of cigarette smoke.

'Ivan, I mean. Don't you think?' she said. 'It's a bit . . .'

She'll say she felt she could hear his heart, or a heart, beating and the thought of what it must be like for a pair of identical twins, one of them dying, only really struck her then. She'll tell how she had a ridiculous urge to hold on to Guy, to grip him so as to hold him there, as if doing so would stop him from floating away, would stop the same thing from happening to him, or perhaps to let him know he, Guy, was the one that was still alive, that the feel of her would do all that. All this made her think of DNA and blood and cells multiplying and dividing. It made her think about babies and of how simple the process was to disconnect. Donna and that baby of hers drifted into this dream, and Alison will talk about thoughts that flickered like a film of how they both existed as separate entities, really, now, yet they'd once been linked together, Donna and that baby of hers, tied together. And she'll say she thought how easy it is to break that tie. She'll say she thought then of her own babies – unborn – and she'll say she thought of them as wounds, separate to her, almost, but not quite, personified organisms.

'Are you worried?' Guy said – this Guy she'd manufactured beside her.

She'll say she was aware of shifting about a bit, unable, quite, to get comfortable in that single bed.

'Are you?' she said, and she felt like she raised herself up so that her face was above his. She'll say she was stroking him, stroking his face, his neck, and his skin felt grainy, thick. 'Are you worried?'

He wasn't looking at her. She'll say he seemed to be looking for something hidden up in a corner of the room, or that damp patch on the ceiling, or the map. His muscles were rigid. She'll say she wondered if there was make-up on that skin there, if there was powder or blusher or something.

'I need to tell you something,' he said.

She'll say how he seemed to take a breath, like an opera singer does, how he shuffled upright. She'll say it became a terribly vivid dream – this was the place for that, an inbetween place between the real and the unreal – that she was

54

sure of actually guiding it herself, of hearing his head bump against the headboard, of sensing him swallowing, of seeing the swallow happen, his Adam's apple a large mobile stone in his neck, of making her Guy do all this. She sat up, too. The air was vibrating, she remembers.

'I already know,' she said, because she, at that moment, she thought she did.

There were footsteps, and she woke – she made herself wake. She was probably unsure of where she was for a couple of seconds, what the map on the wall was, what the stain on the ceiling was. She'll say her eyesight was blurry with the dream still, but she saw a shadow flickering across the gap at the bottom of the door. It hesitated, then went.

And she swung her legs off the bed, and she'll say it was like the link, the tie between her conscious and her unconscious, snapped, and she knew she'd have to go downstairs. When she looked at the fingertips of her right hand, she'll say she saw they were bleeding, probably from clawing at the mattress.

※

Alison will say that when she got downstairs, Donna was standing next to the sink, biting the side of her thumb, spitting bits of skin out of the side of her mouth. Her cheeks were not quite scarlet but not far off. She was looking around her, around the floor, like she was looking for something she'd lost, or had just woken up herself from a strange dream and was trying to make sense of something. At first, Alison will say she thought she was holding a cuddly toy, the baby's perhaps. Flood stood close to her, a spume of smoke haloing him. Neither said anything or even looked at her.

On the floor, a cat was quietly giving birth. Flood's crystal glass seemed to shimmer an odd light against the worktop there.

'No,' Donna said, very quietly. Just that one word.

Alison will say she felt large, standing there, she felt conspicuous, like a large, red devil, but they were ignoring her.

'Woe betide you if you don't,' Flood said, and he threw his cigarette into the sink.

Alison will say she remembers Donna shaking her head.

'Give it 'ere,' Flood said. And Alison will have seen then that Donna was holding a kitten. 'Give it.'

The cat on the floor trembled, let out a short low-pitched growl and stood up. Another kitten was being born, its glistening head appearing suddenly. The other two kittens flopped about on the floor like wound-down clockwork toys.

'Right,' Flood said. And Alison will say she remembers this clearly: he stooped down, his joints clicking, scooped up both of the kittens in one thick-fingered hand. Alison will say she remembers the length of his fingernails and the yellow on the fingers of his cigarette hand, and the stain on the crotch of his trousers. He seemed to catch her eye for a second, less than that. His eyes, she'll say she remembers, were like murky water. When he went outside, he left the door open, but she would have only been able to hear, not see, what he would do. Donna seemed to see her then and the creature in her arms still shimmered.

'He ain't havin' this one,' she said. 'This one's mine. I'm keepin' this one.'

Her cardigan was greasy, her hands were. The kitten squirmed, blind.

From outside there was the sound of water and metal. There might have been other sounds, too.

'What's he doing?' Alison said. 'What's going on?'

Donna wouldn't, or perhaps couldn't, say. She might not have been able to find the words, and Alison will tell how everything seemed suddenly silhouetted against the way the light fell.

When Flood came back in – and it was only moments later – his hands were wet and he said something Alison didn't quite catch. He stood looking out of the window, as if he was collecting himself, as if he couldn't let himself exist in any other world than this one here. But he was holding back, and she'll say she got the feeling that if she hadn't been there, it might have been different.

Greebo came in, looking flustered, Alison will say there was blood on his shirt.

'Goin' to need some help with this ewe,' he said.

Flood, she remembers, scratched his neck, and it made her recoil. She couldn't move far, or will say she didn't feel like she could, and anyway, was afraid of breathing some of that air in. Donna and Greebo, she'll say, shifted closer together – a mating dance, she'll say she thought.

'Where's our Guy?' Flood said, and everyone looked at Alison.

'I don't know,' she said. 'Out. Maybe walking?'

Alison will tell how Donna let out a laugh, but it was a laugh that didn't belong there, it belonged in a pub, or a party.

'I honestly don't know,' Alison said. 'Honestly, I don't.'

Alison will say she remembers Flood wiping his hands on his shirt, across his belly. She doesn't remember hearing the door in the hallway open, but there was a smell wafting in, of decay or a full septic tank, perhaps, and a sense of footsteps, familiar, creaking floorboards upstairs that, at the time, she thought might have been her imagination. Flood sighed the longest sigh, went to say something, but didn't. Greebo said, 'How about the ewe then? What we going to do?' Flood looked down at his feet as if they might give him some kind of answer. The house was making sounds and Alison will say she thought it might have been the weather, the wind was working up. Greebo shook his head and left, and Flood seemed to twitch, like he was losing power. He seemed unsure where to go and stood by the door looking out towards the hallway. They will have all heard how pronounced his limp was as he climbed the stairs.

Then it was just the two of them: Donna and Alison. Donna sat down, placed the kitten on the table. It was the runt, shivering and still damp, a cheap fairground toy look about it. 'You *do* know,' she said, watching the kitten leave a little sticky path on the table. Donna, according to Alison, was lumpen, awkward, just then, but she moved a chair away from the table with her foot and motioned for Alison to sit. Her eyes were wary, Alison is clear on that, and she said, 'And if you don't know, I'll tell you.'

But, see, Alison did know. She'd known all along. In her heart, she did. She must have.

☙

Alison will say that later, when she'd asked him, Guy, how he felt, after seeing his brother lying there, his identical twin brother, he changed. She'll say she thinks he lost his temper with her, that his whole demeanour changed, his face did. She didn't, quite, understand. She's frightened of him, of course. Normally. Who wouldn't be? But this was different. He was different, here.

Which is, probably, how he'd come to be walking.

And this is important.

Everywhere here there is a sense of loss, but, if we ask him about his, I bet he'll tell us, eventually. Walking those old paths of his, he must have felt something old, something from his old self move within him. It must have been – surely to God – palpable, despite everything. You can't come back to this place – he can't, somebody like him can't, that is – without feeling it. Everything contradictory, everything sliding into, or out of, some kind of mental discomfort. All other feelings pushed aside, all of them, pushed. What were those feelings? Grief? Anger? Guilt? No. Too simple, all of them. Whatever they were, they would have been pushed, shoved, into the thinnest of membranes. So thin, in fact, that surely, *surely*, what had been distributed around his whole body for years, as a dense, painful fog, was now being rallied or somehow evaporating, and what was left, what it was going to reveal, was a tender ache, or better, an agony.

At least that's the hope.

Guy, see, Guy had been many things, but he was a wan-derer. He *had* been, that is. In the past. All those years ago. Drifting through this place here, he used to say, had taught him to understand certain *connections* between the internal and the external. This directionless drifting served a purpose for him. It pulled him out of himself, for a start, or perhaps pulled the outside into him. His pace, generally, he was unaware of, as if some detachment had taken place between his mind and his body. He used to say, in the old days, how he'd tell himself that he was no longer Guy Flood, he was someone else. He was no-one, or he was Ivan instead, because even though Ivan was his almost-double, his almost-doppel-gänger, he had no idea what thoughts went through his twin's head and so interiors didn't matter then, only exteriors, and he could let his mind drift, let his body stagger if need be, and as he would let all this happen, it must have seemed to him that all his despairs, all his worries, all his wrong-doings, floated away. Easy as that.

Imagine what it must have been like for him being back here after all that time, into the interzone of the Black Country. Imagine it now. Imagine him feeling as if he'd passed through some kind of portal, back in time, into a different time-system. Imagine the place re-engineering itself into him, of him feeling like he was becoming – or actually becoming – a kind of interactive thing, not man-made, not nature either, but something yet to be discovered. Imagine him, if you can, the way the place was working on his mind – nothing coherent, nothing easily *explainable* – and think of the power of it, his allegiance to the place itself, how he would have been thinking that whatever had happened in the past, however the past had treated him, he was aligning himself, twinning himself, with something that was even more forceful, more dynamic, than that past, that treatment. Imagine a slow curve of a line made entirely by walking ahead of him. Imagine him being gradually, no, suddenly, *aware* of, rather than hearing, specifically, the sensation of water, the grey-green blades of grass, the complexion of nettle leaves, and the meaning of yellow in the fennel flowers, the curiosity of a lump of concrete or cement. Think about how the rhythmic placing of each step might become something out of his control, as if he was being drawn into the place, or back into the place, or into something, like he was part of its permanent essential essence. We could guess that he thought of himself as Guy then, Our Guy, and that all sense of time evaporated along with his feelings, so that, together, what he was sensing was bodily, like utter relief, beyond satisfaction, as if he was in the process of finding the answer to a long-asked question he hadn't even realised he was considering. It's at times like that when it's easy to believe that the gaps between feelings and thoughts are actually as important as the thoughts and feelings themselves, that there is no concealing anything, and that having recognised this, life – his life – could be changed for ever. Ask him where he was, or where he walked to precisely, and he can't tell you, because there were moments of erasure so that he forgot, or didn't even recognise where he was and what he was doing, yet it all seemed easy, painless and easy, and looking at the landscape, to him, looking at the canal, the factories, it looked like a foreign land, like a myth or a dream, as if he had burrowed into his own unconscious, where there was a clear picture of what and how he needed to be, what he needed to do. But imagine this, imagine seeing this, experiencing it – because you can bet he did – words, he'd say, emerging through the bark of trees and slipping off the leaves there, like blossoms, like memories; words and sentences shimmering on the surface of the canal water, appearing like living creatures, like gifts, through the water starwort. It's God's country, he'll still say, this place here.

Imagine that. Imagine him believing that he had reclaimed this place. Imagine him thinking he could just pick it up and put it down whenever he felt like it.

Ask him how he ended up back at the farm though, and he won't be able to tell you, exactly. He'll say he doesn't recall even entering the house, let alone seeing anyone, perhaps he might vaguely remember the state of the outside with its cracked concrete slabs and bucket of dirty water, but he'll say he doesn't remember seeing Flood or Greebo. He must have been deafened – anaesthetised – by the walk, or so he'd have us believe. He'll say he ended up in Ivan's room. He'll talk about the dressing table against the far wall there. It is an old, walnut veneer dressing table, dusty, tatty, stained by mugs or glasses or bottles of scent. Brass flower-shaped handles have gone brown, like petrified wood. It has a huge egg-shaped mirror, dirty and smudged with finger-marks. It was his mother's, originally. Its mirror was the one in which he'd first seen a reflection of himself. He'd often talked about that, not to Alison, of course, that first proper sight of himself. He might only have been two or three years old. Imagine the surprise, the disappointment in seeing such familiarity staring back out at him. He might have thought it was Ivan he was looking at, or a warped version of him, and he might have tried to reach through and perhaps couldn't work out why he couldn't touch this other almost-self. Imagine him now, looking at himself in that mirror, realising, perhaps, or seeing himself as a composite of his parents. That colouring was Flood's, and he had his mother's eyes. He *has* her eyes, that is. But there were differences between him and Ivan that perhaps only they could see. The obvious one was the side they parted their hair, for a start, mirror images, you might say, and certain expressions were only *similar*, to him at least. He used to say he remembered the fascination he felt, looking at himself in that mirror there, realising that he and Ivan were, in fact, *alike*, and that the knowledge that they were twins might make some people see them as more alike than he did. But what would we have seen? What would we have made of him? A grown man, yes, care-worn, yes, a furrowed forehead, eyes – his mother's, yes – slightly blood-shot, a promise of a full head of pure white hair, like his father's. Had he been crying? Even he didn't know, or certainly wouldn't admit. We might say he looked older than he was. There was definitely something hyped-up, over-wary about him, as if he was burgeoning with something.

Ask him and he'll tell how he sat down at Ivan's desk, about the copy of the novel there before him, its black cover like a black hole into the past. He'll tell about the notepad, the paper of it browned by age, and the pencil, hard and sharp. He'll tell how he sat there and wrote, how he pretty much filled that note pad, about how the words poured out of him, like water, coming from God knows where. He'll say he realises now about the gate he left open, and the muddy footprints through the house, and about the handwriting written so quickly it didn't even look like his. As he recollects all this, you might be able to see a flicker of this moment of flow: the pencil writing by itself, or seeming to, the words flowing, the sentences, unhampered by anything, a secret unstopped. And he was thinking – he *must* have been thinking – I can do this, I *can* do this. Imagine the feeling he might have had. He might even admit that it was almost as if he was being lifted onto a slightly different plane, or being swept out on an easy tide, or, better, was on the upsweep of a flame. Imagine him feeling like it was one of those times when he felt ahead of the game, just one step, but ahead nonetheless. Alison will say he told her he'd done it, written it all down. She'll say he looked saintly as he told her. Saintly. Guy, the saint of horned animals, labourers, people with epilepsy, protector of outbuildings. But. Alison will tell that as soon as Flood appeared at Ivan's bedroom door, as soon as he realised Flood was there, Guy recognised he was beginning to *try* to write, and he'd instantly lost his footing with it, as if landing back on earth after having been effortlessly soaring slightly above it. And once he became cognisant of how difficult he'd recently found writing, he'd recently found *being*, once he'd somehow stopped floating slightly above his task and had become embroiled in it, stuck, heavy with emerging feelings, Alison's opinion is that he realised the difficulty. He *became* the difficulty. And those few last hurried lines of his were apparently badly written – even the handwriting flowed differently, more recognisable as his own. Perhaps he became aware of his wrist aching, his fingers. Perhaps he noticed the thinness of the paper and started to wonder whose notepad it was – surely not Ivan's? He would have been surfacing back into the now so fast, even the walk he'd done earlier might have felt like he'd imagined it.

Imagine Flood saying something. Something like, 'Guy, what d'you think you'm doin'?'

And the room, the voice, everything, would have taken that situation back twenty-five years. More. Maybe Guy said something, Alison won't tell, but we can imagine how he closed that notepad, and we can imagine he felt crippled, as if his body had somehow crumpled, as if part of his life had been snatched away while he blinked. Alison will admit that she heard, from the kitchen, Flood say something about wasting time and losing the plot, about 'that woman downstairs'. And Guy must have slipped the notepad and the novel into the drawer.

Which is how Guy came to try and find me – us, and how Ivan's room came to be gutted by fire.

❧

She won't be able to explain it, Alison that is, but from the very beginning, she couldn't quite find the right frequency here. She just couldn't tune in. She couldn't catch hold of the sensation of the place, or deal with the feel of it. She'll tell how she'd read somewhere – or perhaps Guy had told her – that the enclosed towns of the Black Country have a city's landscape and a village's culture. Still, she'll say she lay down with him, Guy, on his single bed. It was the middle of the afternoon and they'd never done that before, lie down like that in the day. The north and southbound rhythms of the distant M5 motorway must have sounded like the sea, but ask her, and she'll say she lay there feeling marooned, stranded. Guy lay awake next to her, still holding the pencil, and the tips of the fingers of his other hand tapping her elbow in a way that made her skin crawl. She put up with it for half an hour, more. Sometimes her need to please weighs heavy. Flood was downstairs in the kitchen talking to Greebo. She'll say she could hear. She'll say that when she sat up, Guy touched the back of her neck, she felt it, she felt him. For something to say, she said, 'What's going on downstairs?' and, 'Are they arguing?' This was how they came to find out about what was happening with the farm.

There was the tail-end of a conversation fading when they got downstairs, and Alison will say she felt like they'd interrupted something important. She'll tell how she felt for Guy's hand like a child might.

'All right?' Guy said to everyone, and she'll say she heard it, his accent, like a sound that had been struggling to come out for ages.

A pan of water was boiling on the Aga and flames there turned from orange to purple and back again. The air was sticky. Flood squinted over at Guy, then sat down slowly at the table. The chair creaked under his weight.

'And now there's him, here,' he said, flicking his thumb towards Guy.

To Alison, it maybe looked like Greebo wanted to say something to Flood. He wore overalls that were too big and there were stains, oil, it looked like, but others that Alison wouldn't know. The longer the silence went on, the more irritated Flood seemed to get.

'So, is it twelve o'clock tomorrow then?' Guy said. He was talking about the funeral, and Flood nodded slowly.

Greebo sighed, they all heard it. His hair, Alison saw, had been scraped into a thin, darkish pony tail, his face was a map of lines, though she'd only seen one particular expression on it and wondered how that happens, all those lines like that on a face like that. He could have been a hundred years old, she'll say. Flood seemed to sense something because he made the slightest movement, more like a jerk of his chin, and Greebo picked something up off the side, a torch or something, and left without looking at Guy or Alison.

'If you'm hungry, you'll 'ave to wait a bit,' Flood said, and both Guy and Alison said something about not being hungry at all.

Guy sat down, and then Alison did.

'You all right, Dad?' Guy said, and Alison will say that, just for a second, she felt like she saw the Guy she wanted to know.

But Flood's hands clasped and tightened into a fist, she'll say she saw him do it, she saw the skin on his knuckles thin out. And she'll tell how she saw the brown envelope, the tip of the letter, on the table in front of him.

'Well, we shall have to be all right,' he said.

Alison will tell how she saw Greebo outside hesitate and look in at them through the kitchen window. It seemed like he stood there for a long time, looking in at them like that, and it seemed to her that she was the only one who noticed it.

'An' you?' Flood said. 'What am you doing? Still working at that paper, I suppose.'

Alison will say she couldn't work out if this god-like man was angry or sad, or what. She heard Guy take a sharp breath in.

'Yeh,' he said. 'The newspaper, yeh.'

'Just as well,' Flood said. 'We'm finished here.'

And he tapped the brown envelope and sighed. Alison will say she could still see the dampish marks on the table where the kitten had been put.

'Compulsory purchase,' Flood said. 'Summat about building a road. A bypass or summat.'

The pan on the stove was spitting water, and Alison wanted to turn it down, or off. There was a telephone, a grey one, attached to the wall and when it started ringing, it was more a relief than anything. Flood's breath rasped as he stood to answer it. They both, Guy and Alison, heard him say something about stock and feed. Outside, Greebo seemed to be looking for something, staring out across the field, Alison will say she could see him. There were storm clouds on the horizon, she felt them – she'll say she did. And the pan kept boiling and boiling. It made the air smell sour.

When Guy and Ivan were kids, they looked more alike, except for the hair, but there wasn't really any telepathy between them, nothing preternatural like that. At the first primary school they went to they were put into different classes and Flood went up there and shouted at the Headmaster in the main corridor about that. There he was, this giant with wellingtons who, when he went, slammed the door and left great muddy footprints on the wooden floor. Ivan cried, but Guy did not, when the Headmaster spoke to them in his office. They were placed in the same class after that, told to sit right next to each other. Even though they were young, they started styling their hair the same way, deliberately, which made it more difficult to tell who was who. They liked this, the boys did. Occasionally, during class registration, both would answer to the same name, or not answer at all. They did it because they could, or perhaps to see if they could. And because the teachers didn't like it. One night when they were about seven years old, Guy decided to shave off all his hair if Ivan would do the same, using Flood's razor. Guy told Alison he remembered the feel of Ivan's hand on his shoulder, steadying him and drawing the razor up and over the crown of his head, and doing the same back. He remembered the itch and scrape of the metal against his scalp, the hair, like a dead animal on the bathroom floor. Paulette nearly killed them when she saw them, heads like two peculiar eggs. Flood took the belt to both of them. But it made it impossible for others to tell who was who. It was the thing they had that others did not.

At school, other kids got to take the class gerbil home during the half-terms to 'learn responsibility' and as a treat, but the twins weren't allowed. Paulette thought there were enough animals on the farm as it was. At school one playtime, Guy told Ivan to put the gerbil in the toilet to see if it could swim. They went to another primary school after that.

Guy only remembers this part of his life in fragmented bits and pieces, or at least that's what Alison will say.

᪡

Not much later, Greebo came back into the kitchen, said the ewe had died, and so had the lamb. They were all in there: Alison was still sitting there, and Donna was there – she'd put the kitten on the table again and it swayed and fell about in front of them like a drunkard. Alison will say she remembers looking at Guy and seeing a different version of him, slightly altered. It might have been the light in there. She knew Donna was watching them both. Flood was talking to someone on the phone, trying to get a decent deal for what remained of the flock, trying to sell off what was there. Listening to him, she'll say it was like witnessing someone who'd never used a phone before. He shouted, lost his way, got irritated, scratched at the back of his neck. She'll tell how she glanced across at Guy, wondering why he didn't offer to help, why he didn't intervene. Instead, he stood up, motioned to her to come to him, which she did. And while Flood battled with the telephone conversation, Guy said, to nobody in particular, that they were going out.

Of course, he'd told her about something that had happened years before - he'd told her what he'd wanted her to know - and as they walked down the lane and on, past the river, past the canal, she thought about that, or at least she'll say she did. What you need to realise about Alison is that she doesn't fear mistakes, if anything, she's thrilled by the possibility of them. See, he'd told her about this pub he'd been a regular in - we all were. He'd started going in there when he was fifteen, sixteen, but nobody had ever asked him his age, of course, not round here, they still don't bother with that. Besides, everybody knows everybody, anyway. He'd been, Guy had, well known as someone who could handle himself in those days, working on the farm had done that to him, that's true, most of the others worked in factories, in steel works or foundries. But he was tall, muscular, handsome in an uncultivated way, and there was this sense of potential about him. And he'd been known as a bit of a lad, he had a mouth on him, and he could drink. If there was any trouble - everybody knew this - that's when the landlady there, Deanna, would give him the look, and he knew he needed to step in, sort it out before it went too far. Outsiders, punters causing trouble that is, were basically animals, and didn't expect it of him, so the element of surprise was the thing. Pubs, they're like farms, actually.

Alison thinks she knows all this. She thinks she knows everything about Guy, but the truth of it is he stopped going in that pub a couple of months before he left, just a little while after that time there was that lock-in.

Alison will say she knows that. She'll say Guy told her it was the landlord, Derek O'Boyle's, birthday. The big four-oh. He was a big man, Derek was. Fat, to be honest, obese. Morbidly. Smoked Hamlet cigars. Liked a little dab of Charlie now and then, the odd pill. Deanna had laid on a spread: sandwiches, pork pies, black pudding, crisps, that kind of thing, cheap poor-quality feed, for Derek's birthday, and had invited a few regulars to stay on, had sorted some music.

Now, the story Guy would probably have told Alison is this: it was before Paulette had died, of course. Guy had already started spending more time away from the farm and much more in the pub. That night, the music they were playing was old stuff, disco stuff, and it was starting to irritate him. He'd had a few pints himself, obviously, and had managed to cadge some pills from Derek. He felt for them in his pocket a couple of times, making sure they were still there. And the atmosphere, or what he felt was the atmosphere, was good, happy. Derek was dancing, holding a couple of pork pies, one in each hand, a big gummy grin and that bit of hair he usually combed over was flapping about next to his ear.

'Hey, chap,' Derek said to him. 'Come here.'

And he'd grabbed Guy and kissed him hard on his cheek.

'See this chap here?' Derek shouted to the crowd. 'I loves him, I does.'

And Guy believed it – he's told Alison this, he really did, at the time.

'If I had a son, I'd like him to be like our Ivan here,' he said, and he lifted Guy's arm, squeezed his biceps. And then, close to his ear, ''course, I'd settle for *son-in-law*.'

Deanna leaned across the bar, slapped Derek's arm, said, 'That's *Guy*, you yampy sod, not Ivan. Open your eyes.'

'Guy. Ivan. Whatever,' Derek said, hugging Guy hard. 'This one here, he's the good 'un.'

Guy will have thought he knew exactly what he meant, it wasn't the first time he'd heard this, and he'll have felt proud, big, like an overperformer, just hearing it. Deanna slid a pint of mild across the bar.

'Her ladyship's upstairs,' she said. 'Might grace us with her presence in a bit. Her's waiting for Ivan, but perhaps her'll come down if her knows Guy's here.'

A couple of the men wolf-whistled and called 'Roseanne! Roseanne!' and 'Get down here!' And Derek waved the sound away. Guy, being Guy, will have most likely felt a bit coy, a bit embarrassed. He'll have told Alison that, anyway.

'Come on, here, chap.' Derek grabbed Guy's cheek. 'Come and have a drink wi' me, for me birthday, like.'

Everybody cheered. And everybody was very drunk.

It was springtime, it's true, but as hot as summer. Everybody would have been sweating cobs in that pub. Men were dancing, but you could smoke inside then, and so, after a couple of pints, they'd have all looked like blurry holograms. What will Guy have told Alison? That he'd gone to the Men's, had taken a long piss and had had to steady himself against the wall to keep upright while he was doing it? That a harmless breeze from the open window was welcome, a bit of a waft of damp metal in the air, probably from over Tipton way, and maybe silage, smoke and something more sickly-sweet? He might have told her about how an owl or a fox cried out, like a human voice, and how he looked up and out of the window, about seeing the trees out there shaking like boxers at the ready, or lovers, maybe. He might have told her that. But what about this? Would he have told her this: that when he turned round, Deanna was there, leaning against the closed door? He probably wouldn't have realised until then what the shape of her was. She was plumper than he'd imagined her to be and she was wearing red stiletto-heeled shoes. He'd only ever seen her behind the bar until then, torso only, and perhaps his first thought was that she clearly wasn't very tall, looking at the heels. Four inches at least, those heels, and still she only reached his shoulders. Not very tall, and plumpish, and also a little bit pissed. Her legs – he'd definitely remember them well – were bluish-white, mottled with something, a bit like a certain type of egg-shell, like a carrion crow's. And she was smoking a cigarette in a way he'd never seen her do before, letting the upsmoke float out of her mouth, smother her face, or part of it, and seeming to breathe it back in somehow through her nose. The way she was doing it gave her this unbeautiful, intense kind of look, like a shark emerging from dirty water. And then she said something like, 'We won't be missed' and 'Do whatever you fucking-well like.' But she was swaying a bit, presenting herself to him like some kind of condolence. So, in fairness to him, perhaps it would have been easy to push her against the sink, or the urinal, one or the other. She would have been a little bit like a rag doll, like a sedated thing. Between us, he'll have probably thought there was something, what? Seductive or teasing about realising her skirt was plastic, not leather, and that what he expected would have been firmish flesh underneath was, most likely, more like the feel of a deflating balloon. Something about her hands being dry and cold against him, and a smell like dogs and sugar around her neck and shoulders might be information he'd keep to himself. Her eyes were strange, too, and only later did he realise it was that she'd lost one set of her false eyelashes. But – and this is what he would have told Alison – he tried to be quick, and the sound of 1970s disco music – what was it? 'Love Train'? Something like that, and shouting from the bar was filtering in like a big joke, anyway. Perhaps he'll have told Alison that he tilted his head to feel the breeze from the window, focused on the outside there, the brick wall, the glimmer of barbed wire, the peculiar yellow of the security lighting, those trees – how old were they? Hundreds of years? Thousands? Alison will have imagined how he had to really concentrate. The music, though, was making the floor vibrate. Imagine him having to really think, really concentrate. Imagine him thinking that now: just concentrate. He'll have had to hold onto her tightly, Deanna, he'll have had to hold onto her wrists to keep her in some sort of position so that she would stay on her feet, stop her from swaying or shifting her weight. Perhaps he'd have been thinking about the arch and stretch of her back. Perhaps he'd have had his eyes closed. He was probably worried, he must have been, that his pills would fall out of his trouser pocket – tiny pills they were – and be lost in the gaps in the floor tiles, or crunched under her red stilettoes. And if she said anything, it must have become just a sensation of something against his flesh. Actually, though, he didn't embarrass himself, never mind how much beer he'd had, never mind the noise from the bar, or the possibility of being interrupted or found. Never mind any of that. In the end he wasn't even out of breath, he'll probably have told Alison that, anyway. And afterwards, he will have told Alison how Deanna

73

smoothed down her skirt with one hand, how she'd have lit a cigarette and held it in the cup of her hand, how she took one single drag from it before flicking it onto the floor, how she said, 'You look pleased with yourself,' as he washed his hands, though his reflection, blighted by the flicker of fluorescent lighting, would surely have said something different to him. The floor still vibrated with the music from the bar. And, he won't have told Alison this, but he'll have thought it might have been motion sickness he was feeling just then.

'Come on then,' he said, he whispered it. 'We'll be missed.'

'I don't care,' Deanna said. 'Do you?' And she was putting lipstick on, glittery pink stuff, gurning at herself in the mirror, gurning at him, tapping her stiletto heel against the tiled floor like she might be about to dance, right there, in the men's toilet.

'What's wrong?' she said to his reflection, and she was adjusting her skirt or her knickers, and her eyes were a strange pearly blue.

'Nothing,' he said. 'Nothing's wrong. At all. Nothing.'

And then she said something, and Alison will say that Guy has memorised this. She said, 'She's upstairs. You'd only have to go up there.' And she turned to face him, lifted her chin like she was ready to be kissed, as if she burnt on, undimmed by anything, and she said, 'Like mother, like daughter.'

Perhaps she might have intended to smile at him, or move over and kiss him, and perhaps he'll say he was hoping to *God* she would not, but half-way through the chorus, somebody cut the music – he will have told Alison this – and then all he could hear was a sudden upshouting of male voices coming from the bar. He'll have told how he looked across at Deanna, searching her face for a meaning, watching her expression change, watching her give him the look. They probably left that men's toilet with more synchronicity than they'd have anticipated.

See, he'd have been expecting to break up a fight, some daft, drunken shambles about football or women or horses or money or drugs or dogs. He'd have been expecting to bowl in, grab a couple of idiots and drag them apart, maybe drop the nut if need be, get Derek to unlock the door and boot them right out. He was probably expecting a free pint out of it – God knows he'd have needed one just then. He wasn't expecting what he saw.

Which was Derek, out cold, on his back on the floor, looking like some kind of distant mountain range, very still, bluish. He wasn't expecting the posse of blokes at the bar, hopping from foot to foot, jibbering and fumbling about, clearly unsure what day it was, let alone what to do. He might not have been so surprised to see a couple – three or four – of white lines of powder on the bar and a couple more on one of the tables.

He'll have told Alison that when they saw him, the blokes at the bar started talking at him all at once. Words slurring around at him. All very confusing. He knew he needed to call for help, he knows that now. One of the blokes, Greebo, it was, looked like he'd had his nose dipped in icing sugar, said, 'He's dead, man. Is he dead? He just died. Like that. Stopped breathing. Like that.' And he snapped his fingers and sniffed and coughed, all flesh and powder and wisps of smoke.

Deanna, inept, was down on the floor, slapping Derek's face like she was some kind of Nazi officer. Guy watched her stoop down, her ear against Derek's chest. A single half-eaten pork pie was being squashed under one of her knees, the straps of her stilettoes were cutting into her ankle, the greyish roots of her hair were suddenly there, and, of course, the red marks on her wrists as guilty as fingerprints. Her legs looked streaked with something. The air in there was sharp – it smelt like petrol, or maybe ether – something chemical at any rate. Motes of something floated about in the air. Deanna, looked at him, her lipstick, smudged so there was this clownish look about her.

'Do summat,' she said to him, she screamed it, like somebody on a fairground ride. 'For fuck's sake, get our Roseanne, somebody!'

He might not have told Alison this. He might not have told her how he looked at Deanna's neck and the shape of her pulse there, fast, or that when he took a step back, when he looked around at the others standing, wiping their noses on their arms, pinching their nostrils and coughing, looking at Derek like he was some kind of vision, he felt a sudden indignity of unwanted responsibility. Maybe he had a thought about the ewes on the farm and listening against their chests, and maybe he thought about his mother, Paulette.

Maybe that is what he'll have told Alison.

But running across the carpark, clambering through the broken fence of the beer garden, and out through the Japanese knotweed towards the canal, he'll have heard the sirens and if he didn't see, he'll have imagined the blue lights, but he didn't look back.

And he didn't go back to his bedroom in the farm, either. He wouldn't have wanted to wake people, Flood in particular. Instead, he locked himself in the caravan. Greebo didn't live there yet, and it was grim. Airless, sealed, like a killing jar, it was, or like the inside of a camera, and he couldn't, or wouldn't, open a window, or even open the curtains, or flick on a light, or light a candle – certainly not light a candle – for fear that the air in there contained something invisibly flammable. He was surely soon soaked in sweat, what with having run from the pub. And he'll have lay down there, listening, unable to stop his thoughts developing, but hearing only the odd car in the distance.

Often, voices travel along the borderlands here like indecipherable announcements at a railway station. Often there's a hum, low, like a distant drill. Perhaps that was how it was that night, for Guy. You can bet the soles of his feet felt hot from running, as if he'd got glass in his shoes, or smouldering coals. Even then, even lying there, lips on fire with dryness, tongue parched, he must have been able to *sense* it, this place all around him, closing in, like a dog might sense a threat, or another dog. And there is such a complicated sadness about that, isn't there?

But that was a long time ago. Of course, he'll have known he ought to have helped, but that wasn't the worst thing he'd ever do, not by far. And it was years ago. Years. And this was to be the first time he would go back there, to that pub. It's as if he thought that this place here forgets, or forgives.

Alison will say she was curious, anyway, and she walked there with him. She'll say she felt like the stranger she was. All seemed alien to her, even the grass, the tarmac, the water in the canal. Even the birds sounded extra-terrestrial. And the place, when they got there, the pub itself, seemed to her to be medieval. She'll say it was very quiet, empty but for a few Eastern Europeans congregated there, drinking at the bar, looking like locals might. Of course, Derek and Deanna still keep it. Deanna, behind the bar, has changed her hair colour. Red, it is. And, later, Guy would tell Alison that she'd lost weight, and height, that something was going on with her face that was both familiar and unfamiliar. But then, there, that first moment, walking through into that bar, Alison will say that Derek seemed planted on a bar stool next to the till, still fat – fatter, actually – a 'Vote Brexit' T-shirt barely covering his belly, his fingers gnarled with arthritis, holding a chipped mug of tea. To Alison, it must have been like watching a scene from the past as Guy asked for a pint of mild and she watched them all, but Deanna especially, trying to compute. It was, Alison will say, pitiful. So pitiful, it seemed that Guy had to put them out of their misery.

'Guy,' he said. He told them. And then when that seemed to make them look even more confused. 'Flood. Guy. From the top farm.'

Deanna seemed to understand first and her face changed. When she put her hands on the bar to steady herself, Alison will say she noticed the way the skin of her arms hung, like a sail almost, at the top there, the triceps, or where they used to be.

'Guy Flood,' she said. It was a statement, like someone calling a register. The Eastern Europeans shuffled to make room for him, but their side-eyed wariness seemed to put him on guard.

Alison will say she was fascinating, this Deanna, this queen of the Black Country, underneath all that age. Her face, the skin of it, rippled, like it was a separate entity, unable to decide what to do.

Derek said nothing. To Alison, he seemed to be trying to focus, like an old dog might. There was some inexact movement going on with one of his hands and his posture was unusual.

'Pint of mild, I said, Deanna,' Guy said, and he leaned against the bar. 'Please. And a half.'

Alison will say she remembers clearly that Deanna didn't even look at her, not then, she just started pulling the beer, and Alison will tell how she caught the smell of it, watching it gush into the glass, dark like something out of a sewer. She made it look like a dance move, all of that, Deanna did.

'The half in a ladies' glass?' she said, without looking at Alison and without waiting for a reply.

Alison will say she remembers that behind the bar, behind Deanna, there was a glass bowl - crystal glass - with bags of pork scratchings, and there were cards with little bags of nuts hung up like an advent calendar, a picture of the slim midriff of a girl showing; there was a wooden chopping board with sliced-up lemons and a sharp knife, a plastic ice bucket, behind which a plaque that said 'Best Black Country Pub 1998', and there was a foxed mirror which made Guy's reflection look somehow artfully arranged, like some kind of vulnerably aroused animal, as if he'd practised it. When she looked at him, Alison will say Guy was smiling, and something about the light meant that he seemed taller, god-like. She'll say she remembers thinking: he's glorious, thrusting, unswerving – he's like the distant canal. Just then, she'll say he could do no wrong, that she thought she would die for him. She'll say she felt as if everyone in that pub was looking at him, waiting for his opinion. But she'll also say that outside, through the window, she could see the landscape seemed vast suddenly, and it was darkening. Shadows moved like strange maps on the bar top.

When Deanna put the glasses onto the bar, it was with a flourish, like she was presenting him, Guy, with a precious gift, like he was lucky. But she leaned forward, Deanna did, and Alison will say the skin of her cleavage wrinkled like newspaper, and there was a sound like acid rising in a stomach, and without taking her eyes off Guy, Deanna spat a long ghost-shaped blob into his beer. The glass was wet with condensation, some of the froth overflowed. But Guy didn't move. He did not. And Alison will say that everyone watched – everyone – as he never flinched, he didn't even blink. He just picked up the glass and drank a full half pint, probably more than that, before putting the glass back down on the bar so gently it was like it was something to be treasured. He didn't even hesitate, and he didn't wipe his mouth, and his lips gleamed. According to Alison, Deanna watched him particularly closely, her eyes darting over him fast but her body very still, unnatural.

'Guy,' she said. She purred it, a proud statement. And this seemed to break a spell and the atmosphere changed. The men at the bar re-animated, got on with talking and drinking. But Deanna leaned further forward across the bar at him. 'God, you've changed, I wouldn't have known you.'

Alison will say she felt a bit under surveillance and felt herself in the beginning of a blush.

'You've really changed,' Deanna said. 'You don't look like yourself.' And she was planning on touching his face, that was easy to see, her hand was advancing towards him, each finger with a different gold ring. Alison will tell how he took it, Deanna's hand, gently, and fixed that smile of his on her.

'Must be the good air, the sea air,' he said. 'And the love of a good woman.' And a little frown flickered across Deanna's face, just for half a second, and he had hold of her hand, and they stood like that, like they might be about to arm-wrestle. To the side of them, Derek was watching all this, and Alison will say she heard him speak. 'Guy Flood, well, well, well.' And Guy, still holding Deanna's hand, and without even casting him a glance said, 'Still alive then, Derek?'

And Derek seemed to shudder, and Alison will say he turned his head, and the flesh under his chin trembled, and she thought he might just topple off the seat, and he said, 'Yeh, I am. And so's our Roseanne.'

Alison, even now, will say she hadn't realised why exactly they'd gone there, until then.

They didn't stay long. Obviously. Alison will just say she followed him, Guy. She'll tell how she remembers the way they walked along the towpath, along the curve of the canal, and something about the quality of light there seemed to give off a mood ring of colour that seemed blocked between the trees and the dip. She'll say she watched him, the way he was walking, like he was walking an old well-trodden path, old footprints into which his fitted. She apparently watched his walking reflection flicker across the surface of the water, a dark ghost. In places, she'll swear she could see his reflection creeping even deeper across the silty floor of the canal. Just here, the earth is sodden, the towpath, it can't seem to swallow, is the problem. Its muscles are clenched.

Further along the water, in fact, there are factories that look like they have risen out from the depths, and at certain points of the day or year, smoke from the chimneys makes the scene look like an Edwin Butler Bayliss painting, but Alison wouldn't know that. From the lower reaches of the hill, though, she might have thought the farm looked already partly flattened, slightly tilted – italicised, really – against the landscape, against the sky, on a mound of green, like some kind of salve to the urban heat island around it. She might have thought it all looked unreal, two-dimensional, very slightly sinister, as though, perhaps, it was already haunted, the scaffolding a jumble of pipework like a giant spider's web. At least, this is what she'd probably say, like she's trying to make it something it isn't. Walking closer though, she'll have surely been able to tell how, it – the farm – looked squat, ugly, that the gutter had detached itself or was sagging, probably with the weight of leaves and water and mud, yes, but more than that. There was a peculiar mist, which probably didn't help, and what she will say is that she purposely kept her head down, climbing that hill, watched each step she took through the mulch on the driveway. There was, she'll say, a smell of, or a feel of something damply hot pressing towards her like something powerful, like a fever, like a rot, like something terminal developing. She would describe it like that, like a tumour, perhaps. And outside along the house, when she looked, she'd have noticed that there was ivy or some creeper – she must have – or the scars of where it'd edged and died off. And that the concrete paving was cracked, and that there was a patch of nettles that might well have once been a herb garden, and that there was a blocked-off path that might have once led to the back of the house. And that a line of small, silent birds were sitting on the scaffolding, and that the remaining sheep were forming a horizonal murmuration across the curve of the top field. All of this, she'll have – she must have – noticed for the first time.

The side door of the farm was unlocked, but the damp had done something to the wood of it, so Guy had to shove it hard with his shoulder, and it jarred across the floor. One of the dogs skulked in beside them, its coat long and caked with sand-coloured mud. It looked up at her, panting, its eyes like a man's. She'll tell you this. And she'll admit that she felt a surge of sadness. She'll say it was like a sudden heat, the effect was so shocking. She might have had to steady herself, one hand against the wall. It was Donna, her voice, that would have brought her – both her and Guy – back to the now. She called something from the kitchen, she shouted, and Alison will say it sounded thin, her voice, it didn't sound human. It must have seemed so odd to hear Donna's voice just calling like that, that it must have occurred to Alison that Guy might have been taken back to when Paulette was there, perhaps, to when he was a lad. And she'll tell how he ran, or had broken into a run – it was a short hallway – and had stopped dead at the doorway to the kitchen. Donna was leaning against the worktop, holding something around her hand, holding it like you might hold a baby, a tea towel or rag of some kind, it looked like. There was a growing patch of something on the material, that on first sight, might have been black, like ink leaking from a pen. And Alison will say she remembers Donna standing there – such a strange, intimidating stance, it made her want to laugh, so she'll say, but she won't mention the baby, Alison won't, how she thought it was him she was holding. She didn't move, Donna didn't, but she glanced at both of them briefly, and then looked at the floor. Her feet, they would have been able to see, were bare, dirty – she seemed to be on tip-toes, teetering on the edge of falling.

'Christ,' Guy said. 'What's gone on? What's happened?'

He was still standing in the doorway, trying to work out how best to deal with it. Alison stood behind him, breathing against his neck.

And she'll say Donna held out her hands towards him – towards them, as if reaching for a life-raft. Beneath the heel of her foot, when she looked, and all round the floor were irregular shards and splinters of glass, shimmering like diamonds or white hot coals as if she was standing in a furnace.

Automatically, Guy moved towards her – he was still wearing his boots – and beneath his feet, the crunch set Alison's teeth on edge.

'Here,' he said, and he grabbed Donna's hand.

'Sorry,' she said. 'Sorry for shouting like that.'

Guy was looking around, trying to work out what was best to do. Alison will say there was blood on his shirt somehow, and when she looked, Donna's feet were perilously close to slivers of glass. There was some movement, some rushing forward and sideways, such a strange unco-ordinated dance, with Alison trying to help Guy, probably, though actually the way she'll say it, it's as if she's obsessed with the nearness of him. Of course, she is.

.'I tried to pick some of it up,' Donna said. 'That's how I did this. I just dropped it, I don't know how, I was only doing the washing up,' she said.

Alison will say she remembers she sounded different, beseeching.

'Christ, is it his crystal glass?' Guy said. 'It's not, is it? Is it Dad's?'

And Donna didn't answer. Alison will tell how the voiceless movement of her jaw made her look obscene, like a mannequin.

Close to – that close, anyway – Alison will say, there was a smell about Donna. Something meaty, something carnal that Donna herself was surely cognisant of. Alison will say that Donna turned her head, half-embarrassed, half-disappointed, and that she was shaking, her arms were. Guy seemed to know how to handle that, and Alison – all of them – must have heard the glass crunching beneath his feet as he lifted Donna up. They all must have heard her gasp against his neck. Alison will tell how he placed her, Donna, like an ornament, onto a chair at the table, that he didn't seem to know what to say exactly, so just shook his head and started unwrapping the towel from her hand. She resisted, at first, weakly, but it was easy to see she didn't mean it. She was like a child, and

84

Alison will say she wouldn't have been surprised to see that her feet didn't touch the ground, sitting there. The injured hand, though, the palm of it, she could see was fine, but it was the thumb, the very tip had a jagged gash, like a little yowling mouth, and tiny beads of red emerged, grew and dripped, before their eyes.

'Did you wash it?' Guy said. 'Did you wash your hands? They're filthy.'

Donna's eyes were closed, she was swallowing hard.

'Hey,' he said. He was holding onto her wrist, and Alison will say she could see how tightly he was holding her. She'll tell how she could imagine the feel of the sinews there, or bones, or something grinding together under his fingers. He said, 'Is it clean, this?'

'I don't know,' Donna said.

'You don't know?' He didn't even try to hide his impatience.

Donna opened her eyes, and when she looked at him, it was as if she was not completely focused, like she was loose-eyed.

He ran some warm water from the kettle on the Aga into a dish, took it over to the table, and plunged her thumb into it. She yelped and he squeezed her wrist tighter, said, 'Stop that. It's not even hot.'

And she did, straight away, stop it, that is. Alison will say he looked over at her as if he was seeing her through a glass pane or a seventh veil. And Donna, she'll say now, seemed trapped in an uncertainty of fear and anger.

'It was only an accident,' Donna said.

Alison will say that when she stood back and looked at the scene, Donna looked like a drifter, sitting there at the table like that. And what else did she look like? She'll say she could perhaps see Paulette in her, around the eyes, or what she'd imagined must be Paulette. But the curve of her spine was the same as Flood's, and the impression was that at any moment she might spring out at you. She looked dirty, too, unwashed, and Alison would have wanted to tell her that, like a parent might, but she did not. Instead, she said, 'I'm sure it doesn't matter. It's only a glass, isn't it?'

Donna glanced at her, and Guy did.

'It was *his* crystal glass, Alison,' he said. And he shook his head and his expression changed, she can't quite describe how.

There was a broom next to a bucket of dirty water, and he set about sweeping up the mess.

Alison will say she watched all this, and he must have known she was watching his every move. Donna sat like a ragdoll at the table, where she'd been placed.

'He'll kill you, you know,' Guy said. 'He will. He'll go fucking mad.'

And he was sweeping the glass into the corner, and he was doing it angrily, really quickly, missing bits. It looked, Alison will say, like a precious mess.

Donna was holding her thumb tightly, against her mouth, watching Guy. She has this way of looking about a hundred years old, and Alison will say she said something. Perhaps Guy didn't hear her, or perhaps he wasn't meant to. Anyway, Alison heard her. Apparently, there was blood on her lip, Donna. And she leaned forward, and said it again. She said, 'You shouldn't have come here.' She whispered it, to Alison. 'Why did you?'

Guy emptied the pieces of glass into the bin, his whole body, grim. Alison will say he stood for a while just looking at the bin, what was in it. And she'll say Donna said, 'Why, really?' so quietly, looking back, she's not even sure if she imagined it or not.

And then Guy turned. He didn't look at them, and he let his arms drop, his shoulders, his voice.

'If he asks for it – Dad, I'm talking about – if he asks you for his glass, tell him...tell him I did it. Tell him it was me.' He sighed. 'Unless you can think of something else.'

Donna nodded, as though to say 'What else is there to say?'

'What else is there?' she, in fact, did say.

꩜

It wasn't late when they went up to bed, it just seemed late. Alison will say she'd felt dirty and wanted a shower, but there wasn't one, and there was no hot water, or she couldn't seem to work out how to get any. In the bedroom, when she went back, still dirty, Guy was sitting on his bed, naked in the dark, his back to her. When he turned, the layer of pale hair on his chest glistened. Neither of them spoke. There seemed to be an abnormal quiet. She'll tell how Guy's clothes were on the floor, as if they were something contaminated that he'd thrown away. She'll tell how she watched him, and how she thought, then, about the first time she'd ever seen him, how he'd been homeless, a hopeless case sleeping rough on the beach wearing most of the clothes he owned and carrying the rest in a battered backpack. She'd bought him coffee, to start with, had felt sorry for him, then had felt something else. She'll say something about how he was honest with her about himself, but she doesn't seem to like to give details, except this: quite soon he moved into her flat, but his way of being able to withdraw from her or into himself, whichever – to distance himself, let's say – made her feel as if she could live or die on her own account, and it wouldn't matter to him. He had this way of making her feel like a deliberately unwatered plant, and that made her feel panicky, made her open herself up to anything he might want to tell or do.

87

Remember though, that she doesn't fear contamination, actually she's thrilled by it. And, listen, we know that eventually, he told her a lot. He must have. What is hidden from her isn't worth knowing, probably.

Here, now, seeing him back at the farm, she'll say the way he speaks is different. She can't explain it, or won't, but she'll tell it's something in the way he says 'Black Country' as if . . . as if, what? The sound of it makes him feel something he isn't conscious of? Perhaps.

Anyway, she'll tell how she watched his body in this boyhood bedroom of his, and how he climbed into bed, coyly pulling the duvet up to his chin. She'll tell how she undressed quickly, how he said, 'Close the curtains,' and she'll say that when she looked out, the landscape was stretched dark, a grey lid, and lights flashed like distant lighthouses near hills she didn't yet know the name of.

The curtains didn't quite close, there wasn't enough material, but, in any case, not much light came in. She'll mention that in bed, the flesh of his thigh against hers felt cold, like polished glass. And she'll say that as they lay there staring at the ceiling, both of them, the weight of the wind down the chimney caused the map on the wall to gently flap.

She's clear on this though: she'll say that she knew she had him, that he was hers, and that she wanted him, and she wanted him to know that, to feel it like an oncoming omen, to feel it as if he was the most wanted man ever. But this want was hampered by the way he sometimes was – he was then – unable or unwilling to want back. And when he was like that, she feels – and she'll tell you this – *energised*. Not powerful, that's too simple. That's not right. So she'll tell how she turned, placed her hand on his chest – she loves his chest, the contours of it – and he said something, turned his head away as if looking at the partition wall, or something on it. His neck, his chin, she'll say, looked holographic, silhouetted against the way shadow or darkness, one or the other, was falling on the pillow. She'll tell how she lifted herself up, her face close to his, that his face was – is – a map, the contours of which she knows well, but sometimes, like then, that there were areas she knew he didn't want her to go to. But that didn't matter, not to her, and not then. That's not what it, what they, were about. She'll say she could smell him, the old him, on the duvet, the pillow, as if there was part of him that had never left. She'll tell how she breathed all that in, that smell. She'll say – and she would truly believe this – that all women are capable of rapid change, and that she is no exception. She'll tell how she thinks she knows herself well, and that there are certain times, *particular* times, when she could evolve into an entirely different species. Lying there, just then, breathing in the past, she'll have been feeling herself change. And even though she'll admit that Guy wasn't exactly willing, that he said something about being exhausted, that they'd be heard and it would be embarrassing, and that beneath them – *beneath* them, remember – his twin brother, the body of his twin brother, that is, lay – well, it was all her. She'll say she persisted, or rather the thing she'd become persisted, that she cajoled, whined, murmured, and that she felt acrobatic, or balletic, like a professional of some kind. She'll tell how she felt capable, as if she'd grown stronger, grown muscular, grown tentacles, that some dormant force had risen to her surface. It would have become very dark in that bedroom and, of course, she'd have preferred some kind of light, but there's something about a lack of vision, and surely she'll have been more aware of sounds: the sound of the map gently flapping in a draught against the wall; the sound of flames carried up through one of the other chimneys like a pile of voices gossiping through the bricks; water running thin and fast down through the broken guttering outside; the way the wind buffeted the windows and sang through the scaffolding and up and over the roof; the distant gekkering of a fox. And Guy, of course, lying beneath her, which she, Alison, will say just amplified the quality of her longing for him.

Afterwards, she'll probably have told him she was sorry, at least she'll say she did.

And overnight there was a storm. Hailstones battered against the window, and a gale whined through the roof for almost an hour. Both of them, Alison and Guy, must have been lying there awake, sometimes at different points throughout the night. It was the kind of night that makes you listen out for noises in the lulls in between, sure you could hear them. Guy, Alison will say, kept putting his hand on the wall that separated his room from Ivan's – she'll say she thought he was doing it in his sleep at first, and then realised by his breathing that he wasn't. A couple of times he said, 'Did you hear that, just then, that noise?' because they'd have been able to hear the anguished cries of some animal or another, or the distant flow of water. Alison will say she felt the sensation of hearts beating, and doors closing, and a feeling that there was a yearning or a crawling of something in the walls. Half-asleep, she'll say the hailstones against the window were creatures, rats, clambering against the glass, and in the gathering light, she was sure – she'll say she was – that the motes of dust in the air were choking. And that the creaking sound was, actually, the walls buckling and cracking. She'll say she could feel the force of the place. More than once she saw a slow shadow through the gap at the bottom of the door, thinking it was probably Donna, thinking the storm must have been keeping the baby awake, but she's sure she never heard him cry, the

baby. Not once. She'll say she imagined him, this child, cling-
ing to his mother like an animal, for comfort. Just once, she
was sure it was Flood, lumbering past. She'll tell how she heard
him in the bathroom, the sound of him, his urine, hitting the
bowl, thundering out like it might actually be the river. The
toilet, it seemed, had a very weak flush and she'll say how she
remembers listening to him work the mechanism again and
again. And beneath them, in the room directly below, the
body of Ivan lay. Alison will say she kept thinking about this,
about him, the body of him lying there. And when she looked
at Guy beside her, very close, at his face, in half-shadow, in
half-sleep, it was as if he was in the process of returning to
the blackness of space himself. It could have made her weep.
And she'll say at some point in the night she heard Flood go
outside, to work, she assumed, his heavy footfalls fading slowly,
though it was about 5 am when odd bits of bluish light came in
through the gap in the curtains, because of the frost or snow,
or what looked like it, having settled along the thin edge of
those far hills. It was about then, she'll say, that Guy sat up,
got up, and even in that light, she'd have been able to see the
blotches of red on his neck, his shoulders. She'll say she hadn't
realised until then she'd caused them. She'll tell how he pushed
the duvet away and she asked him if he was okay, meaning,
'Where are you going? What are you doing?' He might have
answered, or he might have gone to the bathroom without
speaking. Either way, she'll tell how she lay waiting for him,
aware that another day was starting, that the final filaments of
yesterday had vanished, and how, when he came back, he'd said
something about wanting, needing, to go for a walk, and she'll
say she grumbled, like a child, told him it was too early, that
she'd said, 'Don't worry, let's sleep,' and that, actually, she felt
anaesthetised. This place, here, was making her feel like that.

91

Vaguely, she might have been aware of Guy saying something, asking something, protesting perhaps. Her memory is blurry about this, but she'll say she remembers feeling him get back into bed, the warmth of him, or of him warming up, and she remembers the smell of metal or iron or steel, vaguely sulphurous, because the air here can be like that, heavy, like that, like something man-made. And she remembers being held too tightly, like an urgency of need, and she remembers the feel of needles in his breath against her. And she remembers thinking, if not saying, 'It's okay. It's all okay. I'm not Roseanne.'

✵

If you're wondering what Alison knew, she knew the Floods had farmed in the Black Country for three generations. On the same farm, there. They'd never lived anywhere else. They didn't know anywhere else. They *were* the Black Country, they spoke it, looked it, felt it. Guy told Alison that as a kid he thought Flood knew everywhere here, in this place. He'd told her he used to think that when Flood closed his eyes, the insides of his lids would be speckled with a map of the place. To Guy, Flood was like God, and this place was his country. When Flood called you to his room, or what he called his room, it was like being called to account for your sins.

Alison will tell how Guy had told her Paulette, his mother, was often depressed. She became depressed. She let the depression become her. To Guy, she wore it, this depression, like a scarf around her neck, or maybe a rope. For a year or so before she died, Guy had said she'd changed, the way she moved, especially around Flood. Think of Victorian pickpockets, urchins, the way they might have moved. She moved about the farm like that. That's the way Alison will say she understands it to have been. More and more, Paulette apparently took to erupting with something – not anger, something else, that perhaps neither Guy nor Alison have a word for. And then at other times she looked frazzled, vulnerable, as if however hard she tried to pull herself up, she just ended up feeling invisible, empty with nothing more to give, as if some fucker of a devil was following her about wherever she went. Alison will say all this now.

But listen, this part is important, and Alison will say Guy told her this: that one day, Paulette had been sitting at the kitchen table, her face thin with premature age, worry or whatever. 'Your father wants you,' she'd said. 'Now.'

One of the ewes had had a stillborn lamb. It had been Guy's fault, he'd interfered too much. Flood was in his room. They couldn't afford another loss, he knew this, Guy did, and of course he was nervous. He knew that Flood had given up trying to balance the figures. Paulette used to do them, but had stopped, and Flood had said he thought that Guy or Ivan ought to have taken over dealing with the accounts. Donna was, what, fifteen? Fourteen? Too young, anyway, to ask, aside from anything else. And as for the money, there seemed to be more going out than coming in, Flood had told the boys this. Guy went into the room, his father's room, saw Flood standing there. There was a calculator on the desk there, and he guessed Flood couldn't get it to reckon up the same list of figures twice running, so had given up and was trying to fix the draught that seemed to be coming from the window frame. There was this strange coldness in there. Guy felt it, and the edges of bills and bits of paper rippled and sometimes skimmed the desk and landed like an animation on the floor. The window frame was rotten as a pear, anybody could crumble some of it away easily just by touching it, and it wasn't the only one – it wasn't the only problem with the farm, even then. Guy knew this. It was like the outside was pushing at it, trying to get in, or trying to push it over. Sometimes, even then, it was like as if the whole place was swaying, coming loose from its foundations. Guy stood, then, waiting. He was watching Flood, the back of him, his big wide back and broad shoulders – wider then than now – knowing he was about to be told about this situation with the ewe and the stillborn lamb, as if he didn't already know about it. There were odd bits of tools on the shelves, a couple of screwdrivers, a monkey wrench, a hammer, and Flood picked up the hammer, and his knuckles looked shiny white, and he looked like he was about to smash through the glass with it.

Alison will say – she will describe – this scene, where Guy stands clearing his throat, or perhaps saying 'Dad'. Whatever. There's Flood, turning round, more like a handler than a father, his desk stacked with papers, bills, a calculator, pens. There's the rotten window frame and mucky glass because Paulette had given up by that time on the cleaning. There's the smell, the outside, maybe it was leaching in: the smell of cooling metal blowing in from over Tipton way, the galvanising tanks. That's the smell. Sometimes it smells the way blood smells. It does. And there they were, both of them standing for a bit, just looking at each other, taking it in, the feeling, the atmosphere in there, everything, seeming familiar and foreign at the same time.

Flood said, 'What happened with the ewe?' And when he put the hammer down on the table, he *placed* it down. And Guy, how did he answer? Well, Alison will say that all in one breath, he told a bit about the dead ewe, and a bit less about the stillborn lamb. Flood, apparently, did not move a muscle, he did not even to blink, because, most likely, he would have been giving Guy the hard eye. Behind him, at that time of year, lambing time, the sky would probably have been swirling with steel, gifted with consciousness, and the view out there, well, it's proper Black Country. Guy stood there, his legs most likely feeling weak, and trembling, maybe feeling a plunge in his stomach, his gut – think about that. So. The lie, when it came, rose like a bubble out of murky, slow-flowing water.

'It was Ivan, Dad,' Guy said. 'He didn't know what to do. I told him to wait for you, but he said he could do it by himself. He interfered too much.'

Now then, think of Flood lighting himself a cigarette like he never even realised he was doing it. And think of him picking up that hammer.

⚘

Alison will tell what happened with Guy and Roseanne. She'll say she knows all this because he told her. She'll say it was Ivan who liked Roseanne first, which Guy had thought was pathetic at the time. For a start, Ivan was seventeen, and Roseanne was fourteen, only just, and she had these different-coloured eyes, one brown, the other blue, as if, somehow, she was made up of different stuff to everyone else, or should have been two different people. She was a tease, a chancer. Nothing about her was normal. Derek and Deanna, her parents, she despised, she'd told Ivan this, and Ivan had told Guy. She'd said she'd leave and go as far away as she could as soon as she was old enough. She'd said she hated this place, this Black Country here, she felt she was too good for them, for this place, she made Ivan speak in the same way, as if she was consuming him, as if he was trapped within her thrall.

Alison will tell how it happened – how Guy told her it all

happened, that is. See, Flood had punished Ivan, because of the ewe and the stillborn lamb, because of what Guy had said. Ivan had ended up with a black eye and a split lip. Guy had let that happen, see. But it had got out of hand. The adrenaline was boiling, after that. It was complicated, very complicated. Everything was upside down in the farm, in Guy's head. Ivan was a mess. Everything was a mess. Guy had had to get out of the house, he'd felt he had to. But, see, he knew Ivan had planned to meet her, Roseanne, and he was running and running, the physical effort sharpened even more by fear, or by expectation – though how could he have *expected*? Alison won't say how Guy knew where to meet her, but she'll tell how Roseanne was waiting – she was waiting for Ivan – just past the aqueduct, where the river intersects the canal, where the two bodies of water flow so differently. Alison will tell how she, Roseanne, was wearing a T-shirt with nothing underneath it as if she meant to tantalise. There were sweat patches under her arms, and at the time Guy wouldn't have even realised that girls could sweat like that. And when she lifted her arms, he could see the little patches of black hair there, as if it was all designed to make him feel something he didn't yet know how to cope with. And Alison will say it was Roseanne who suggested it, going off into the woods next to the canal. 'For some cool,' she'd said, because, of course, she wanted privacy, really, she'd wanted privacy with Ivan. So, Alison will say, of course, Guy had gone with her. Gone into the woods, that is. Why wouldn't he? The smell of warm leaves and the scent Roseanne was giving off must have felt mesmerising to him, it must have been overpowering. This is what Alison will say. And he followed her, and she moved like roots of trees or like the river, slow but strong through into the middle of the woods where they couldn't be seen, where there were

96

only pale shivers of daylight. And she ran, climbing upwards slightly, then down, into the undulations of the way the earth is there, and he followed her. Manhandling branches out of the way must have quickened his heartbeat even more, must have sharpened still more his concentration. And her hair, when she looked back at him, was damp and stuck to her forehead, because that was the kind of girl she was. She had the darkest hair, like an animal's pelt in that light. It would, according to Alison, have seemed like some kind of sixth sense going on between them, between them and that place there, the tension and excitement would have been the same as breaking into a strange building. The drive would have been the same. She was leading him on, Roseanne was, and he was seventeen, remember, and he'd just seen what he'd just seen with Flood and Ivan at the farm, and the smell of wet wood and the sun falling sideways through the trees and the way the trees took up the influence of the space there would have made everything inevitable. Everything. Alison will say she was asking for this, Roseanne was, for all of it, and that she'd have known, of course she would, surely, that it was Guy, not Ivan, wouldn't she? Alison will tell how he, Guy, caught up with her, Roseanne, how he lifted her, moved her, placed her, like a doll, next to a tree, right against it, surprised at her weight, how light she was. Under his feet, and hers, there were fungi being squashed and letting out this dampish, stale smell, it might have been sickening. And she tasted of cheap sweets and salt and metal and she let him kiss her, and her lips felt, to him, like pieces of fruit in his mouth and he, naturally, didn't know how careful to be, he was only seventeen. And he, Guy, he wasn't *him* any more, he was some kind of unregulated entity, and so was she. What was this thing that was going on? It was like all his subconscious longings had suddenly

97

surfaced and surely, *surely*, this must have been what Ivan felt, what Ivan thought and felt and tasted and touched. And it was as if he'd discovered something inexplicable that was there all along and he'd never known. It was greedy, visceral, immediate. This was him, this was Guy being Ivan. It was Guy accessing Ivan's feelings, and he gripped them, afraid he'd never be able to again. Alison will say he, Guy, felt Roseanne catch her breath or laugh or say something, and he slipped, his feet did, because the leaves were mulchy, and he pressed himself against her, and her face, when he glanced, was still and small and strange. He didn't know if this was how it was supposed to be, of course. And he felt like his entire weight was against her, that she was disappearing into the trunk of the tree, that they both were, into the essence of the place, this place, this Black Country, here. He could feel her heartbeat through to his own skin, and he felt her eyelashes flickering against his cheek, and perhaps it was as if their own particular rhythmic elements met, or collided, maybe with the pulsing of this place here, and with everything that had happened. Alison, of course, will say he *wanted* to stop, or slow down at least, he wanted to be *able* to, but everything was irresistible by that time. Everything. And anyway, she, Roseanne, seemed to be letting him slide his hand up inside her T-shirt, and her skin was oddly dry and very hot, like burning paper. Even though she was only fourteen, he was pretty sure it wasn't her first time. Alison will say that because she was a tease, this Roseanne, she put up a little bit of resistance, but that would have just added to the nervous tension, and it was her breath against his ear that did it, her lips against his earlobe. 'Ivan,' she said – was she pretending she didn't know? – and of course, Guy didn't correct her. It wasn't a game to him, then, it was more. It was guilt and fear, the drive is the same, it was a matter of psychology. And, Alison will say, being seventeen, he would have thought, at the time, he was about to die, he would have felt, at the time, his life would have been worth it, and so would any lie, any game, at that moment, because what he needed was to feel something better, something more – he needed to feel like a God.

Alison will say they stayed there like that for only a few seconds, probably, though time, what was happening to it? It was contracting or expanding. There they were, there he was, leaning on her. Whatever it was that had flowed into him, it had quickened, it had vanished, ungrasped. He told of feeling his strength drain out of him, of feeling hers gather. The way the light fell on her then, or the way he perceived her perhaps, she was all nerves and heat with veins like roads on a map. And then, Alison will say, because Roseanne was who she was, it will have been as if what had just happened to her, the full meaning of it, had just occurred to her, because she looked at him then, really looked, really focused on his face. She looked at him, and, of course, he had no energy to even smile at her. No strength. He was trembling, and when she slipped sideways, away from him, he stumbled and had to grip onto the tree.

That night, he lay awake, he felt so buoyed up, and he could smell her on him still, and he liked it and didn't like it, and he would have been able to hear Ivan alive and breathing in the next room – he always could, the walls are that thin – and he dreamed of the canal and the woods, the way the trees were, the way the place was. This is what Alison will tell you.

Back here now, Alison will say she feels what Guy felt. She tries to. She tries to feel the heat of him. There is a sense that she is absorbing the place through him, or thinks she is.

It was still early, and she'll tell how she woke. In the darkness, she'll say she was unsure if she was still dreaming, she'll say she saw him standing there, all head, and she was amazed he could balance. He had opened the curtains and was looking out. She'll say her eyes were open, but he wouldn't have been able to see that even if he had been looking at her. She'll say she could hear him breathing, the pressure and effort of it seemed a heavy anxiety. She'll say she was sure she could hear somebody in the room next door as if memories were embedded, somehow, in the bricks and mortar of the place, but that the whole place was a palimpsest now. She'll tell how she was sure she could hear movement, or breathing, like a violin of noise, despite the hour, and felt panicked. The pillow, she'll say, was damp as if she'd, or he'd, been sweating or crying, and she stayed still, watched him as he looked out of the window. The storm had passed, the hail had turned to rain and fell like feathers, she heard it against the window. There was still electricity in the air, though, and the landscape, the fields, the horizon, from where she lay, looked like a painting by someone very young or very old.

Of course, Guy was very quiet as he dressed, and Alison will tell how he went to the bathroom, how she couldn't stop the speed of her thoughts. The quiet, the night made it worse. And when he came back, she'll tell how she heard him mutter something that sounded like 'Fucking asthma', and it made her tense up and she thought he sensed she might be waking because she'll say he watched her for a bit, and she closed her eyes, imagining his wide mouth with its thin lips slightly open, his eyes perhaps too close together, gruesome. She forced her breathing to even out, and heard him get up again, go, close the door.

But she'll say she heard him hunting about downstairs,

cupboard doors, a sound like an egg having fallen on the tiled floor. She'll say she became aware of the possibility of all movement in the house. Donna or that baby, or as if the map was coming loose from the wall, or as if there was a mouse scratching about in a drawer in the room. She'll admit to feeling a ridiculous panic that he might be about to leave, to leave her, and she dressed quickly, heard the pulling of the door downstairs. She'll tell how she looked out of the window and that, from above, he looked like a constituent of the place, a floating molecule. The sun, she'll say, was beginning to rise but the place was silent as if the cold had driven the birds away and all that was left was guttering covered in white shit and small feathers.

Downstairs, she'll say there were matches and a saucer on the table, grey with stubbed-out cigarettes, and the brown envelope was there too, the tip of the letter was visible, the words 'compulsory purchase' in red. And, surely she would have been thinking about Ivan, dying like that. It was bad enough being a Black Country farmer's son, but dying like he did, who deserves that? Who? And now this. She'll say she knew she felt more clearly than ever then that all the things Guy must have tried to escape from were still here waiting for him, hunting him, perhaps. Maybe it was more of a *sensation* of the place that lingered all over him all the time, and he was just so used to it, he never even realised he felt it. Perhaps she was thinking that we're only ever one layer away from our old selves, that our old selves might have been scraped or washed off or covered up, and a new self is scribed on top. But how permanent is that?

And now, it looked like everything was going, dying or being demolished. Being compulsorily purchased.

She'll tell how she could see him out of the kitchen window, walking out, down across the field, and she put on someone's coat and she set out behind him.

The storm had blown over but the air was thick and damp, still. The sky was a very dark grey lid. It is, she will say, a heavy coffin, this place. And she'll tell how she followed him, keeping a distance behind, keeping out of sight, just following, just watching him. And he walked down the lane towards the river, through the milky mist there is sometimes there. Water in the culvert ran thin and fast. When it's like that, it's as if you can see the bones of it. The River Stour, the hidden river, when he reached it, would have been like a strand of torn grey ribbon. It would have seemed beyond the rain, another time, another generation long gone, down there, not of the now, more like a reluctant slippage into the present. She'll say now that Guy stood, and she watched him, and he seemed to be experiencing it as a vivid, vaguely dangerous thing. It's partly the mud on the riverbank, perhaps. A person could slip and break their neck, this place would let that happen. She'll tell how she hid behind a short wall there, thinking he'd see her, he'd sense her, but he did not.

She'll tell how she felt her boots sliding on something and smelled the cloy of excrement. She might have thought there was a man fishing, but she can't be sure, it might have just been a shadow or her imagination. The flow of the river was fast. Daylight was coming and with the changing light, it seemed a violent orange colour. When she looked back, she'll tell how the shadow of the farm and the caravan stretched long across the field.

She'll say he carried on walking, it seemed without a plan, under the viaduct – some of the paths there are untrammelled – and there are nettles and spikes that catch hold of you – they caught hold of him and of the back of her hand and clung to her clothes. But she'll say he walked on quickly, out, on into the town. The storm had calmed and it had left the place desolate, had ransacked it of its life, and she'll say the landscape looked abstract, a mix of dark colours splattered, wiped across, dabbed out. There was still snow on hills in the distance.

From high up there, she'd have been able to see the arterial roads, only a few streetlights still on at that time, a few very early risers in houses with lights flickering in bathrooms or kitchens, a few shift workers.

She'll say the tarmac felt especially hard under her feet, but Guy had told her all about the mines and the instability of the earth there, and there was a thrill to that, like the earth might rumble, and gravity might rip them both down and away.

The air was dank, gritty, and she'll say she heard him cough as she followed him through the town and on, the breeze sibilant in her ears, the cold making it harder to exhale than it ought to have been and even her lungs were paining with it, but still he'd walked on, alert and not alert, aware and not aware, ahead of her. There are tower blocks next to the ring road, she'll say that to her, they looked like strange works of art or like battleships at that time of the morning, partly lit. She's right. Look at them for too long and they seem to fall towards you. Black bin bags had been piled up outside the entrance and something had torn a few of them open, like wounds, and cans and bottles and vegetable matter had spilled out obscenely. Along the top of the wall next to the flats, razor wire glinted like peculiar Christmas decorations. She'll say she thought it had all been there for too long to be ugly any more, but there's a monstrosity about the concrete there, a monstrous, brutalist pride, that is. The block of flats there is hard-looking on the outside but imaginably soft inside, she couldn't - you can't - help but imagine it. She'll say she imaged Guy might have had a stray erotic thought about that. She'll say she wondered about the people living in these blocks in this place, in this Black Country. Perhaps, she'll say she thought, to people living there, there seems no other world outside of that particular location, when actually, it's just a nook of a whole place. She'll say she was thinking how Guy had lived here more than half his lifetime, yet if you ask him where it is, this place, he'd say, 'It's the Black Country. No one knows exactly where it is, no one. Not even it knows where it is.' She'll say she felt the truth of that just then.

Maybe Alison will tell how someone looked out of the window of a lower-floor flat – a woman – the red curtains the same colour as the light inside. Alison couldn't see properly, but imagined her naked and warm. She waved her hand, this woman, at Guy, or perhaps she didn't. Sometimes it's hard for anyone to work out what is real and what is imagined here.

Down through the old red-brick terraces, through the Old Quarter, across Swanpool Park was a long walk, and Alison would have been in unknown territory. Following Guy, she, and he, had somehow formulated an unspoken, unplanned rhythm, because Alison needed to think, and she needed to follow. She'll say she needed to do it, to shake her thoughts, to think clearly. Guy's brother was dead. And seeing him, lying there like that, had been like seeing Guy lying there. And what would happen about the farm now? Compulsory purchase to build the bypass? What would happen to Flood and Donna and that baby after that? What then? Then what?

But, Alison will say that being there, just walking away from the farm, was like being in a different eco-system, and each street, soused, as they were, with rain, should have represented some memory, some thought from Guy's past. Perhaps, for instance: here, the house of a girl he once obsessed about, and who never knew because they never even spoke; there, the corner he waited on that time, who knows what for; look, the shop that sold bottles of cider to underage kids. Fundamentally, it hasn't changed. None of it. Alison will say it ought to have been like time-travel, walking here, to him. And he looked like he could walk the streets here without even thinking, as if his feet had memory of this place, like a musician has finger-memory. Yet, she'll say, it just felt like a lonely place – it *is* a lonely place – as lonely was behind his eyes, probably.

She'll tell how he had to wait for a bus to pass, the only vehicle on the road just then, how they both waited, Guy and her, though she was way behind him, in the shadows. And she'll tell how when she looked, it was empty, the bus, but for one passenger, his head against the window, apparently sleeping, his breath smeared white against the glass. She'll tell how it made her think of the closeness of sleep and death, just then. Across the road, onto The Broadway, she'll have seen the allotments round the back of the houses there, old wooden sheds, as if nothing physically could have changed for years. She might admit to having watched Guy and his reflection in dark windows of houses there as if he were a stranger, and perhaps she'd say she saw him for what he is: bedraggled, a natural vagabond, with the limbs of a gorilla carrying his own culpability like a heavy suitcase. Maybe she'll have only realised then that it had started to rain again, or sleet. And the noise of it, and the feel of it, maybe gave her a sense of company, as if each drop was cleansing her of things she knew about. And the darkness just there was cotton-woolling her, and she'll definitely say there was a faint sound of metal – a plane in the sky – and it cheered her for just a second, made her think she could, if she wanted to, leave. *She* could.

On, past his old primary school, she'll say he must have been feeling the pull of that incline, that it should have reminded him of his mother, Paulette, being there, and how she used to wait at the school gates – never his father, always his mother. Yet he didn't stop and look, perhaps he even walked a little faster just then. In fact, it was only further up, at the intersection of Sugar Loaf Lane, that she'll say he hesitated, might have thought about turning right towards Kinver, about walking on the Edge, but he did not. Instead, she'll say he made his way back, up through Oldswinford, with the petrol stations flickering into life, and the traffic lights sequencing as if absolutely nothing was wrong. Out again towards Halesowen, past the river towards the viaduct. She'll say he stopped for a couple of seconds, seeming to watch the way the rising sun fleetingly spotlighted through the arches, and she'll say she felt, momentarily, like catching him up, just to be with him there, because it was a strangely beautiful sight, and if she'd been in the least bit religious, perhaps she'll have had something to say about that. But she is not, and she did not. And she'll say he must have been feeling it in his legs, the tendons of his feet, his hips, because she knows him so well, see, she knows the way his body works. And climbing the hill, the farm was like an outrage at the top there. She'll say the whole place was a terrible plea, a rage that felt to her, helpless, a potential ruin. She'll say she heard a dog barking and she dodged the rutted clay soil to miss the puddles in the lane. Day, she realised then, had come like a faulty strip light. There were tracks the Land Rover had made, and she'll say she thought how early it was for Flood to have already gone out. Across the lower field, the remaining sheep formed a weak line and, for the first time, she'll say she noticed a black sheep amongst them, moving as if drawn to her, then changing direction away.

Some way in front of her, Guy had stopped, and was looking at the farm. There were birds, smallish ones, starlings or sparrows, nesting in the gable end, under the eaves. He could probably imagine, if not actually see, the open beaks of a couple, and one of them kept flying out and round and back again up and then under the scaffolding. Coming back, coming back, always coming back. His breath, she'll say, looked like lines of smoke. And she'll say she thought about Ivan then, and the prospect of the day, the funeral, the cremation. She'll say she felt quite suddenly vulnerable, and leaned against the hawthorn hedge, trying to be out of sight if Guy should turn around. The bones of the hedge hadn't yet been fleshed out, but it gave way to her weight, and in places, anyway, the sheep had been grazing on it, so the stiff, projecting branches were, she'll say, like fingers, prodding at her. The sun was cutting through broken cloud, and there were, by then, only spits and spots of rain, and Guy stood for a bit longer, and – why shouldn't he – looked like he was just trying to catch his breath, perhaps feeling like he was sweating it out. She'll say she imagined he'd have felt the fuzz of it, the walk he'd just done, like a bliss, fill his head, fill his chest. And she'll say, with the rising sun, the sky was suddenly like a glowing sheet of metal, and Guy seemed to have to stand and look at it for a bit.

From where she was, she could see him clearly when he walked up to the farm, she'd have heard him struggle with the door, and how it scraped along the tiled floor of the hallway. She'll say she saw him, or a shape like him, through the kitchen window. She'll say she only watched him for a couple of moments. Clouds, she'll say, were purpling, perhaps there was a glint of something against the caravan. It was cold – her feet were, her fingers. It was quiet but for the high-pitched phrases of a song thrush. She started walking towards the farm. Her legs, heavy. She isn't a walker. A vibration of water and mud and earth, and a rattle of an engine disturbed the birdsong, and the Land Rover passed her and parked up outside the farm. Flood was driving. He and Greebo got out and seemed not to notice her walking up the lane, but a moment later they came out again, with Guy. The Land Rover took a couple of goes to start, one of the headlights was out, and when they passed her, she'll say she's sure they all saw her at the exact same second, they must have seen her wave, they must have, leaning in against the hawthorn hedge.

Inside, when she got there, the kitchen was a mess, a couple of flies floated in a chipped mug of tea. The floor was sticky. She trod on something that cracked. Egg shell or glass. Nothing seemed at all clean. The clock on the wall had stopped. There was no heat. The smell of dogs and drains and spent cigarettes seemed stronger than ever, so she'll say she went back up to the bedroom, to get warm, to get away from it. The first light of day was silvering the leaves on the trees outside. Clouds dilated and drifted like jigsaw pieces, and light crept into the bedroom in a way she'll say she's never seen. Like fire. She'll tell how a wave of tiredness caught her off-guard. She'll say she doesn't even remember undressing and lying down.

And perhaps it was only an hour later – less than that – that she woke, scratching her hip bone, her thigh. When she lifted the covers, she'll tell how there were seven, eight, raised red spots. Bites, on her skin there, and there was blood under her fingernails. She was alone. It took her a second or two to realise where she was, that she wasn't at home, so she'll say, and that it wasn't seagulls she could hear. She looked at her phone on the side, but it was dead, she hadn't charged it.

She'll say she remembers waiting, thinking Guy might have come back, but the bedroom felt overbearing, the whole house did. There was a smell of leaking pipes: gas or water. Both. Despite the cold, there was a feel of sweat. She'll say that what she was feeling was like the after-effects of migraining, and she'll say she felt sure that the motes of dust in the air were fine flakes of plaster, and that creaking sound was actually the walls buckling and cracking. She'll say she could feel it, the sensation of the place. And she had an incredible thirst as if she was sickening for something. She hadn't slept for long but she'd slept deeply. She'd had nightmares. She won't say exactly what, but they'd left her with an overwhelming feeling of loss. The skin on her face felt scaly with dried tears. Perhaps it was then that she decided. She won't say. Perhaps it was then that she looked at Guy's map of the Black Country, that she took it off the wall, folded it and put it into her backpack. Perhaps it was then that she went into Ivan's room again, and took the copy of *God's Country*. Perhaps it was then that she looked out of the window at the sky, milky along the anthroscape that is Black Country. Perhaps it was then that she'd have been able to hear the wings of birds clap, clap, clapping across the yard, across the field.

She'll tell how she went downstairs, how the place seemed even more deserted. The door to the front living room was closed, and she was glad about that. The smell of spent candles lingered just there, in that part of the hallway. She'll say she called Guy's name, hoping he'd be back from wherever he'd gone with Flood and Greebo, she'll say she went into the kitchen. It was dark in there, and she flicked on the light and it flickered for a second. In the weak light it cast out, she saw that there was still a sink full of washing up and all the mess. There was still no heat and she'll say she felt her skin prickle. The female cat, so as not to be bothered by the tom, had placed herself in the gap between the Aga and the fridge, where she had crouched down on her haunches, dozily watchful and occasionally swallowing in dry clicks. She'd brought in a fledgling, a starling or sparrow, had left it under the table, and surveyed it from where she was. Alison will say she imagined how the cat would have seen it, this fledgling - the last in the nest, perhaps - flutter, and had known, had *sensed*, that is, that it was not going to be able to sustain flight, or if it was, that it would land not far. A cat has patience that humans do not have, it's true. Most humans, that is. Alison would have imagined this cat might have carried the fledgling, still alive, in through the cat flap and had probably marvelled at the excitement, at the feathers, at the smell of the thing. The thrill, for a cat - as it is for certain places - is in the *experiencing* of the power that holding something captive can create. Alison will say she was thinking all this, so it might have been the cat who heard the latch, the sound of boots being swiftly wiped on the rush-mat. She probably would have recognised the sound as that of Flood, though it might have surprised her that he was moving so quickly.

It was the three of them, who, when they appeared, looked drenched. Guy's hair had darkened and flattened against his head, his skin was pale milk and poppy seeds. Alison will say he looked shocked, as if he'd forgotten she was there. She'll say there was something going on with his breathing she'd never noticed before, like something was stuck in his throat, and a little flicker of something happening about his eyelid. Flood said something, but not to her, and walked the length of the room to look out of the window. There was mud still caked onto his boots so he left footprints like some kind of desire path across the lino. She'll say he stood awkwardly, like a man on a boat, trying to keep balanced. Greebo sat down at the table, a look she can't describe on his face. It was, she'll say now, as if she wasn't there.

'It's Donna,' Guy said, but she's still not sure who to. And she'll say she remembers him changing, his *countenance* changing, his strength running out, like he'd suddenly become ancient. 'She's gone.'

'Her 'asn't *gone*.' Flood was looking out at something through the window, it was like he was distracted by something. 'Her's just *wandering* somewhere. It's what 'er does. 'Er *wanders*.'

Alison will tell how he leaned heavily against the worktop, stared out.

Guy sighed, went and stood by him.

'Look at the sheep, Dad,' he said. ' Look at them.'

Flood made a noise from deep down.

'Look,' Guy said, but he wasn't looking out, he was looking at Flood. 'They're all skin and bone now.'

'They eat. They'm eatin' now,' Flood said. 'They eat the Shepherd's Needle.'

Guy shook his head. Alison will say she'd not seen him like this.

'That's not Shepherd's Needle, Dad,' he said. 'That's Hemlock, that is.'

Flood moved, he lumbered away and sat down opposite Greebo at the table. He said, 'Ah, it's only the roots that am toxic.'

'No.' Guy followed him. 'No, Dad. Look at them.'

Alison will say how his pointing finger looked purplish with cold. 'They're nervous, they're trembling.'

'That's what they do, chap,' Flood said. From one of his pockets, he fetched out a half-smoked cigarette and was trying to strike a match against the table. 'Or have you forgot what it's like, tending sheep?'

'I haven't forgotten.' Guy was talking over him, Alison will say. He was leaning over the table. 'I'll never forget. How could I?'

He dragged a chair up close, Guy did. Alison will say his knees knocked against the table leg.

'What about spraying?' he said. 'When will you spray them?'

'We do'n spray,' Flood said. The chair creaked as he sat back. 'We dip. We allus 'ave.'

Guy sighed out so deeply, Alison will say a plume of dust or ash spiralled up off the table. Greebo, she'll say, was stiller than a corpse.

'You know you shouldn't be doing that,' Guy said.

When Flood stood up, the chair fell backwards. Maybe something of it, or him, broke.

'Am *you* tellin' *me* what to do now?' he said. 'Am you?'

Guy's eyes, Alison will say, flickered like a candle flame.

'That's the way we does it,' Flood said, each word louder than the one before. 'That's how we've *allus* done it.'

Alison will say Flood's face slackened and it reminded her of a slug, treated with salt. He walked over to the window again, his breath thick and catching, his hands on the back of Guy's chair, then on the worktop, like he couldn't stand without help.

'See out 'ere. See. There's everything, chap.' His mouth was wet, his lips were. 'Spiders, beetles, caterpillars, voles, mice. Snakes, even, an' all.'

Alison will say it might have been the light, but she was sure there were beads of sweat on Flood's forehead. He didn't stop looking out of the window. He said, 'This place 'ere though, now, it's gettin' torn apart. Houses, bypasses, ring roads, stuff bein' built over.' His cigarette was unlit between his fingers. 'I used to stand 'ere – and my Dad did, and his'n – and we'd think nothin'd ever change it. Nothin'.'

Greebo, Alison will say she remembers, looked at her like he was beseeching her not to speak. But she did.

'Where's the baby?' she said. 'Where is he?'

Guy was, by that time, leaning against the Aga, shivering. 'Gone,' he said. 'They both have.'

Alison will tell how Flood struck a match against the palm of his hand, lit his thin cigarette, and it flared for a bit and then went out. She'll say it was not so much the fact that he did that, or the smell of the smoke, but more the way he did it, the way he held the match, then his cigarette, the way he stood blowing smoke out against the glass of the window. When he turned round, there was a bit of something, tobacco, or blood, on his lip. He coughed, and Alison will tell how the tip of his tongue was visible.

'We'll have to go and find her,' Guy said.

But Flood didn't move.

'Dad,' Guy said. 'Are you listening?'

Flood kissed the end of the cigarette a couple of times to get it going again and waved the drifts of smoke away. A hint of something, not a smile, ghosted his lips.

'Will she be...?' Guy started asking, but Flood pushed himself away from the worktop, his shadow only very briefly falling across everyone in turn.

'You'm forever doin' that,' he said, squaring up to Guy, or seeming to. 'Thinking you'm the big "I am".'

Alison will say the two men stood like that, as if something might flare up at any second. But Flood took a big breath and stepped back. Alison will say he looked almost yellow as the mottled light from the lightbulb cast out across his face. Taking aim, he threw his cigarette across the room. It landed in the bin.

'You go an' look for 'er if you want,' he said. 'I'm staying 'ere.'

'Dad,' Guy said. 'For Christ's sake . . .'

Alison will describe Flood's face, as if something had ignited. All colour returned to him, blazing red.

'Watch your mouth,' he said, and his voice seemed to erupt from somewhere very old. 'I won't say it twice.'

And he sat down then, clasped his hands together like he might start praying at any minute. Alison will say she's sure she saw his eyes tearing up. He said, to no one, to everyone, 'Them sheep out there, they know their hoof. It's here, chap. Here. And I know it an' all.'

Guy, Alison will say, swallowed, and she heard it. He moved – no, not moved, leaned – forward.

'There's no hay in the barn, Dad,' he said, he whispered it, so Alison will say. It didn't even sound like him. 'You didn't get any in the summer?'

Flood, face blank, but somehow focused, seemed breathless – at least, that's what Alison will say now. She'll say she could hear it, his breathing, like something that was too heavy or from somewhere too deep or too far away.

'Bad winter coming,' Guy said, softly. 'What're you going to do for feed?'

And Alison will say that for a moment she thought there was something, a point of balance, or something between them.

Flood sat back heavily, and the chair rocked. The air in the room was thick with the smell of him.

'You can't just keep takin' off the land without putting summat back,' he said, and his eyes were big and he seemed rooted to the spot.

Alison will say she left them, she had to. Perhaps it was then that she decided. She didn't say anything, she just left the room, went upstairs, first to the bathroom, and perhaps what might have been the first glimmer of an idea came to her then or she might think she summoned something up into herself. She'll tell how she turned on the tap so she could feel the water, so she could feel something that was moving, changing, escaping, so that she could feel the surge of it. Maybe she wanted to wash the idea away. The water ran cold for a few moments. Vaguely, she heard the boiler igniting and rumbling and she'll tell how she had an urge to do something then. She splashed water against her face, her neck, and she'll tell how she held her hands in the flow of it until it was so hot she couldn't continue and the tips of her fingers reddened like she was holding fire. There wasn't a towel so she'll tell how her hands stung as she dried them on her jeans. She'll tell how she went into Ivan's room, drawn by something she can't, or won't, describe, but still. Perhaps she leaned against the desk, pulled back the thin curtains to look out across the field at this wounded place. Perhaps she looked out of the window and perhaps she could see the scaffolding and perhaps it felt like that was the thing that was holding the building up rather than the other way round. Perhaps she caught sight of the sheep, just a few of them, grazing on whatever they could. Perhaps she thought about what Flood said about them knowing their hoof – knowing this was their place. Perhaps the notepad caught her eye again, the scented candle, the pencils in the jam jar. Perhaps. Perhaps she even lay on Ivan's bed, listening and not listening to what was being said downstairs. What she would say is that there was a smell in there, like dead air, of mice, maybe rats, other rodents. She'll say she didn't know then what it was exactly. She probably does now. But, she lit the scented candle, is what she'd say, and she placed it back on the desk, near the window, and she moved the curtains – she drew them closed.

She'll say she wasn't in that room for long. That's as much as she'll tell. Guy was calling her, saying they needed to go straight away. She scooped up her backpack, and downstairs, was met by only the whirr of the lightbulb. Guy, she'll say, looked burnt-out. There was an inexactness to him, a veil of some kind having been lowered. Both Guy and Flood rested their hips against the worktop, looked outside, but the distance between them had grown. When Guy moved, cigarette smoke floated in supernatural layers. Alison will say Flood, though, did not move. She'll say he didn't even look like he was breathing any more.

So, according to Alison, they made their way out to look for Donna and the baby – Guy, Alison and Greebo. Alison would say that Greebo went one way, down through the woods, and she went with Guy, out towards the canal. She'll make it seem like it was an unspoken plan.

She'll say now that she and Guy made their way through the yard, past the mess – there are always chains and ropes there, and generally speaking, nobody notices the blood on farmland, but Alison would say that she did. She did then, anyway. Still, they made their way out down the desire path. She'll say she remembers a line of birds sorrowing on the dry-stone wall, a strange light raking across the field there. She'll say she thought about the making of that wall, of hands, scarred and callused and bloodied against stone, and then realised that there was something undeniably human about parts of the landscape here as if some bits of the anatomy of it were fixed into place, yet others had been invaded, reshaped by revolution. Where the farm was, to her, would have seemed like a secret location. When she stopped to look back up at it, she'll say it seemed blurred out, somehow, a spectral, superimposed thing. And if there was any sign of Flood at the window, she couldn't make him out.

'Why have you brought your backpack?' Guy said. But she'll say she ignored that and just asked, 'Where are we heading?' And Guy said, 'We'll just let the walk carry us forward.'

Weather was starting to obscure what lay before them, and Alison will talk about the waxy corrugations of the river, how the water glowed and scratched at the bank seeming to think it could do whatever it liked, and how the ribbons of light from somewhere were trembling through the trees. She'll talk like this, like it's human, this place, and she'll tell how she could feel the past beneath her, the coal mines, the sewers, layer upon layer of change and sameness. She'll say how it felt like the clay had sucked all the warmth, the life out of the place, and the river had washed it away. She'll tell how she imagined Guy and Ivan playing here in these woods, hiding and seeking perhaps, building secret dens, finding secret paths and passages. And the more she looked, the more she thought how easy it might be to hide here, and never be found, because who would care? But she'll say she was curious about the way Guy was walking, as if with every other step he was encountering a ghost or something. It must, she'll say now, have been strange for him. Weird. To be back here in this place, with its peculiar perspective and its strange angles. It must have been odd. This was, to her, a forgotten place with its damp wood and mirror waters.

She'll say she felt damp seeping in through her boots as if the elements were telling her to leave them to decide fate. They'd passed the culvert which was rasping and spitting, it seemed to her. Guy went on ahead and she'll keep saying she thought how different he was here, how, even though they hadn't been here for a full day yet, being here amongst this landscape had already changed the ways of him. There is a different rhythm here, even she could feel it, it's a kind of syncopation that's hard for outsiders to understand.

She'll say she shuddered as she followed him, but not particularly with cold, more like a vibration, like the feel of an earth tremor. There were things – nettles and brambles – that caught her, even through her clothes. Every now and then there were black patches burnt into the grass where, she'll say she imagined, kids had lit small fires because of boredom. The air, she'll have noticed, had a weak whispering to it, like a chorus of slightly foreign voices she was unable to quite place. She'll say he had his head down, Guy did, as if listening to it, the whispering, like it was music through earphones. It was as if he was oblivious to his surroundings. But *she* was not. She'll tell how a quote came to her from something she'd read a long time ago: something about men not being able to see anything around them that is not their own image, that all things spoke of them, and that the landscape itself is alive. She'll say she can't remember where she read that, but that it seemed right, just then, it seemed about Guy, and about this place, and really, about her.

She followed him at a distance, Guy, partly keeping an eye on him, yes, but mostly allowing herself an awareness of this place. There is a utility to the roads, the pavements, the buildings here, but there is a beauty to them too, their functionality, and she would have approved of that. And there is something else. Guy had told her about parts of this place having roads named after poets. The thought of a place like this, having roads with names like 'Byron Road', 'Wordsworth Way', 'Keats Drive'. 'Poets' Corner', he'd told her the place was known as. She must have noted the anaphoric undulations of grey tarmac and red mud, and the way her footsteps tended to fall into line with Guy's, as if both of them were involved in some dance routine, or were in cahoots. They might have looked like it, but they weren't.

She'll say she noticed the way the cars were parked, with two wheels on the pavement. And the cars themselves were, she'll say, like going back in time. There were Ford Escorts and old VW Golfs. Is this where he had lived? She must have been thinking this. In the past? Was this what his life was?

Each house further on there is covered in grey cement render and she'll say she imagined the feel of that as something tough and unmoveable, unchippable. And each door looks exactly the same. Outside some, there were empty milk bottles, some in plastic crates. She'll say she noticed that there was often the number of the house on the wall nearest to the door, distorted by having been hand-painted onto the render. It looked, she'll say, like she'd imagine communist Russia to look like, not his Black Country, but still. Some had – have – plastic flower pots with the promise of geraniums, pansies or daffodils, and there was smoke from chimneys. She definitely noticed that. She'll have breathed it in, the smoke. Coal.

She'll tell how, further on, Guy stopped, and he said, 'I was born in Stourbridge. It seemed such an innocent place, the mix of forest and factories.' His breath was hot smoke. He looked, she'll say, suddenly blank. If there were faces at windows watching them, that wouldn't have been unusual, and perhaps she'll have seen them and perhaps that's why she'll tell how she put her arm round his waist and when he twisted towards her, she pressed her lips against his and he shivered. She'll say he tried to push her away, but she held onto him. Behind them, opposite the houses, the river tends to flicker in and out of view, and is, by that point, slow and wide like a thick, grey muscle, skimmed with fat from the factories and the air. Men try and fish from it. We call it 'the Forgotten River' and it's full of things just there that it's possible to see, like tin cans, plastic containers, carrier bags tied with tight knots. But there are things that are impossible to see as well. Trees that line the bank are darkened by the clutch of weeds and ivy, held captive somehow by the prospect of rain, and anyway, it's always cold there, next to the river, never mind the time of year. Alison would have felt that, for sure.

Guy said, 'Not here.' And somehow broke loose of her grip, she can't say how, and they walked on, or moved away, more like, and she'll say she had trouble keeping up with him through the labyrinth of industrial corridors and the shimmer of pathways leading to the canal. What would she have been thinking, really? The smell of metal is everything there. And what about the imperfect mirrors of puddles? Walking along there is like walking along a cliff-edge. What would she really have made of that? What?

On further, they will have walked along the towpath to where the canal crosses the river on the aqueduct. It's reshaped, the landscape is, just there. And just there, holding on to the branch of a tree to keep upright, she'll say they stopped. They'll have had to, if only to catch their breath. The river beneath them is only just wider than a stream there, but it moves as if being chased, and somehow its proximity to the canal seems to give it a feeling of panic. Like it needs to rush away, or wants to – if it could want, that is. And it falls and rushes in strange lines, like quicksilver. The canal though, the water, it fools you into thinking it's still. This intersection of water here, with the rushing of the river underneath and the brothy stillness of the canal above is like the past colliding with the present, somehow, or freedom running alongside constraint. And there's a proper sense of risk. You can feel it. She'll have been able to, Alison will. It's hard to explain, that feeling. With the Stour beneath her and the canal alongside, with everything indifferent to her, perhaps she will have been able to smell the way the wood was rotting, or feel the sense of glass in her lungs. Perhaps she'll have seen the way the earth tessellates, always damp, and perhaps she will have felt the movement of it under the soles of her boots.

Alison will say that Guy stood, looking at it, the canal. She'll say both he and the water looked like they had a kind of super-controlled surface tension. She'll say that when he looked at her, his eyes glinted, and she'll say the canal water did, as if somewhere beneath there was a dangerous, virile, supple rhythm, like it might be full of some kind of power. She'll say she asked him, Guy, 'Do you think anything could live in there?' And he shook his head. 'Are you sure?' she said. But he just walked on.

There will have been a sense of the light going, what with more oncoming rain, the clouds being full of it, and she'll say they walked along the towpath, and the puddles were deep and grey. Perhaps they walked beyond the place where the river disappears out of sight, past the weir and the old house, past the place where the alcoholics stand in the gloaming. Perhaps they walked as far as the cutting, where the river reappears yet again, like it's some kind of game, from under a bridge, still rushing, but wider there, as though it's racing from the prospect of danger, but where there's no depth to it. Or perhaps they just stood looking at the debris: the crumpled mattress, the house-bricks, a man's jacket flustering the surface of the water, bloated, puffed up like there was a body was still inside it, and the crumpled metal tossed in there just as if someone had somehow mistaken the river for the canal. Perhaps they stood looking at the bubbles, like thoughts, rising out of the murky water.

Guy said something. 'Where is she?' or something like it, and Alison will say she took hold of his arm and leant against him, and he seemed to let her. The canal gaped, a black laceration, right next to them. There was water all around them, it seemed. She'll say she felt like she was becoming part of the landscape, or it was becoming part of her. Closer, insects were tumbling about just above the surface of the water, and the undergrowth on the towpath was thick underfoot. Walking along there is difficult. Walking there – the *act* of walking, that is – is on the edge of language. But the smell of settled rot, rich and deep and intensely fertile, will surely have been overpowering to Alison. Surely it will have been. She won't say so. She'll say she watched her feet flatten blades of grass and creeping ivy. It must have felt like they were trespassing. She'll say she was suddenly as weak as a kitten, or a bird, or a baby. She'll say she realised that Guy was calling Donna's name. Calling and calling and calling. And his voice sounded like some kind of strange bird. And the water swallowed the sound of it.

꧁

Alison will say she wishes Guy hadn't told her any of this. She does. But she can't unknow it now. Years back, remember, you already know this, there'd been that almighty row about the stillborn lamb and the dead ewe. Bad enough that Guy had lied, said it was Ivan's doing, and Flood had dragged Ivan out of his room and down the stairs, said if he, Ivan, put one more foot wrong – just one more – it'd be Cooper's ducks, that there'd be blood, snot and bone. Alison will say how Guy had just let that happen. What you don't know is that a few days later, Derek came round to the farm, playing his face. He'd brought Roseanne with him. Guy told Alison all this, and that as for Roseanne, the look of her was disgusting, her cheeks were filthy with tears, pale as sin. Alison will say that Guy told her this, and perhaps she was meant to feel less like an outsider, perhaps she was meant to feel like one of them. She'll tell how he said it, how he told her the way that Flood was. Listen to her:

'Wha's all this about?' Flood had said, he'd not long come back from the bottom field, was trying to warm himself in front of the grate in the front living room. Guy was there, and Ivan, both of them, mucky from the lambing.

'I'll tell you what it's about,' Derek had said, and he'd grabbed Roseanne's arm, pushed her forward into the room. 'It's about this. Her, here.'

Roseanne's forehead glinted with sweat and she was trembling, but only slightly. She looked down at the floor. She shoved her hands deeper into her pockets. Her jeans were streaked with something. Strange how her feet shuffled forward when her mind must have been wishing for the opposite.

'Her's only fourteen,' Derek had said, and he pushed her forward and she stumbled. 'Tell 'im,' he said. 'Go on. Tell 'im.'

But Roseanne didn't speak, or even move at first. It was, so Guy had told Alison, as if some odd inner peace had suddenly come upon her, as if, perhaps, the outer shell of her was able to hold everything still.

'Tell 'im what 'e did to yer,' Derek had said, little more than a whisper next to Roseanne's face.

Guy will have told Alison that he wanted to step forward, to take hold of her, to explain, perhaps, but that before he could, Derek had said, 'It was your Ivan.' And Roseanne looked up, at Guy, and maybe he will have told Alison that he saw it, that he noticed something about her eyes, something from somewhere very deep, shining like guilt. And Derek had said, 'It was, wasn't it? It was Ivan what did it to you.' And Roseanne moved her feet like she was kicking a stone away and said, 'Yes, that's right.' And, to Guy, it had sounded like a mix of shame and anticipation.

Nobody said anything straight away, and the smell, or maybe it was the sound, of coal trying to burn filled the room. Alison will say Guy told her, described, how Flood's mouth fell open just enough to show the tip of his tongue, and he turned his head strangely slowly, looking first at him, then at Ivan. It was, so Guy told her, such a strange, intimidating stance, it made him want to laugh.

Almost at the same time, rain against the window had made them all look, see the vast grey sky split through the middle. Guy will have told Alison he wanted to run then, that this was the start of a feeling that was to become familiar, because he knew what was about to happen, or he'd have thought he did. And Alison knows. Guy will have told her. She'll know what happened. And she'll tell how Flood turned on Ivan. This was the last straw, Flood said. She'll say Guy told her about the look on Ivan's face, grey with shock, trying to work it all out, a muddle of panic and hope, and about how Ivan's body, bending like wire, like the kid that he was, was dodging only some of the blows from Flood's backhanders, and how he was saying, or managing to say, 'It wasn't me, I swear,' and how that just made it worse, how Flood was growling, his teeth gritted, spitting, remarkably quick for a man of his age. Terrifyingly so. They were in the front living room, remember, and the coffee table was soon overturned, the sofa was shoved off its coasters. And what was Guy doing? Alison will say he told her, he admitted, he was watching all this from the doorway, from the threshold of the room. Just watching. The fire was trying but became weak in the grate because the kindling was damp and there was too much coal, and Guy watched, from the mouth of the hallway, as Ivan stumbled and bumped his head on the mantel. Alison knows all this. He's told her, and she'll say that Guy probably wanted to tell Flood to stop, or to step in and help his brother, or to admit the truth, that it was him, Guy, not Ivan, who'd met Roseanne in the woods that time. Yes, there was a truth to be told, but Guy didn't, or couldn't, tell it. See, Alison will say he was scared. That's what she'll say. That's how she'll explain it. And watching all this play out, he'd have felt paralysed, rooted to the spot, his mind saying one thing, but his body doing another. Cowardly, you might say. It was only when Ivan fell, his legs buckling in a tangle, onto the hearth rug, that Flood seemed to stop. It must have been vivid in Guy's memory, this, because Alison will tell how he described it, he described Flood, how his breath was heaving, wheezing, how his face was full of colour, how his eyes were dark and wet, the reflection of a fragile flame in them. Alison will ask you to try to imagine Ivan saying something imploring, his voice young, suddenly unbroken, like a young child again, and probably everyone thinking it must be over, surely, that *must* have been enough. What happened to Roseanne wasn't worth this. But . . . But,

Alison knows what happened. She *knows*, or will say she does, because Guy told her. He told her how Roseanne grabbed him, Guy, and her fingers probably felt sharp and small against his arm. 'Christ, Guy,' she said – imagine her saying it. 'Help him.' And you can bet she tried to push him into the room. Had she been stronger, she might have succeeded. But when Flood picked up the claw hammer, when Guy saw him do that, of course he knew he needed to do something, he must have. Roseanne, though, must have just gathered the strength that he could not. Alison knows all this. She does. She knows that Guy saw her, Roseanne, pull back, like an arrow, as if she was preparing to launch herself into the picture, that she didn't shout or scream, and it all seemed to happen at once. One minute Flood was picking up the hammer, the buttons of his shirt open and the obscenity of his flesh, his chest, his belly, was visible, and the next, she was there, Roseanne was, between him and Ivan like a referee in a boxing match, pushing them apart, or trying to. Imagine her, this bedraggled young warrior-woman, like a Viking, her hair falling loose out of the band like drooping tendrils about her shoulders, her eyes blazing greener than ever. She was, apparently, wearing the same T-shirt she'd worn in the woods, the sleeves frayed at the edge. One of her trainers had somehow come off, and her foot was bare and bluish-white with cold. Guy has told Alison all this. Of course he has. It was understandable that he was scared. Ivan had fallen and was cowering and bleeding from somewhere near his eye, his hands covering his face, and at that moment, maybe they all thought that was it, it was over, it was done, finished. Next to Flood, Roseanne looked like the child she was, but Flood was in some sort of flow, some kind of force had taken control of him, perhaps he wasn't even fully aware of what he was doing, or was blinded so much by anger, or what? Responsibility? Power? Or perhaps when he swung the hammer, it was just a case of it being too late to stop. Alison will say that Guy has admitted that he often thinks about this moment, the physics of it, the movement of Flood's arm, the arc made by the head of the hammer. And, Alison might tell how he *did* move forward, he *did* try to intervene, because he said he could foresee – he must have been able to – he could calculate, in that extra-sensory way that people can in these circumstances, exactly what was going to happen. In a split second, he must have realised he'd probably only get a broken finger, a fractured wrist or arm at worst if he'd only managed to get there in time – it was what he deserved, perhaps. He might even have been able to grab Flood's wrist, or the hammer itself and might have stopped it, all of it, from happening, if only he'd been quicker, braver. But Alison will tell that, of course, it was Roseanne who took the blow from the hammer. One, just one single blow. And she'll say that Guy has told her he'd never realised a body could fall like that, as if through a trap door. And he'd never realised, until then, how the sound of bones breaking was exactly the same as the sound of an egg dropping onto a hard floor.

Alison would say she remembers things in fits and starts. Maybe she's telling the truth. The past changes shape even as we look at it, though sometimes even the best of us know we're making up the answers to questions. The past, she would say, has gone, and the future is unwritten, and somewhere in between was a strange present – a kind of simmering, constant untime.

She'll say she was thinking all this as they went out looking for her – not looking for her, but guided by intuition rather than a plan – Donna, she's talking about. She'll say they called her name, and it was like a sacred sound. She'll say the atmosphere was wrong, hushed into a suppressed calm that was as fragile as glass. Further on, there was cat-ice on the surface of the canal and it made her want to walk on it, see if it would bear her weight. She'll say she was sure she kept seeing shapes that could have been a kitten, or a baby, or something in the Giant Hogweed, or caught, stuck, in rushes or knotted by ivy, or sliding like a fish under the ice. Dark shapes seemed to glide by, as if periodically lit by neon, just beneath the surface. She'll say she thought then that nothing is that vivid in real life. All seemed lost there, but living.

And they called and called, and she remembers hearing her own voice echo Guy's or vice versa and it seemed like an insolent noise, the lot of it. There are ranges of hills: Clent, Clee, the Malverns, the Wrekin, sometimes clearly visible like resting beasts not that far away. Eastwards, Birmingham keeps watch. And somewhere westwards are the rolling green-brown plains of Worcestershire. But they, Alison will say, were in the midst of Guy's Black Country here.

Ahead of them, the landscape, she'll say, changed, as if they had walked across some threshold, or through a vortex into another place, a different one. The canal changed and became wider, wilder, the cat-ice gone, the flow of it was visible, still slow, yes, but gathering pace, broiling in the red light of the sun, and she'll say it looked like rust, the water did there, and she imagined it would taste of it, the water. The tips of trees were red and on the opposite banks she could make out the thin, coarse layers of the land – the red-orange rock, and mudstone overburdened with grey soil. Guy, she realised had hold of her hand, in another circumstance, she'll say it could have been beautiful, romantic, even, and she wanted this to last, of course she did, but how could it, really?

She'll tell how she heard him say something – something like, 'This place stinks. Can you smell it?' and she wouldn't have known what to say. But it didn't matter then because she'll say she saw someone, ahead of them, just as they rounded the bend. A woman. Donna. Or like Donna, her hair that deep red-brown, her coat open and her body standing loose – tranquilised almost – next to an aneurism in the towpath, as if she had poached the edge of it away herself. There were horses, two or three, standing like a picture of laziness up on the incline, grazing softly on grass, and she, this woman, was holding an object, white-tipped and still. The breath of her trailed along the canal towards them. Was it her? Was it Donna? Alison will say she couldn't tell for sure just then, the cold will have got to her eyes and the tearing would have blurred things. But she turned and looked at them, this woman. Alison will say she suddenly couldn't remember exactly what Donna looked like anyway, what her face was like. The hair on this woman was too red, perhaps, yes, a bit like Guy's, but what was her face like?

'It's not her,' Alison said. It was, she'll say now, wishful thinking, and anyway, it was too soon.

And then Guy said – Alison will say she heard him say, 'What the fuck are you doing?' And she wasn't sure who he was talking to. The paleness of his face struck her then. Fear-paleness. All colour drained, like skin that would not tan. She'll tell how his cheek muscles sagged, like a dead man's might, yet his concentration was deep and he let go of her hand seeming to forget her and his physical circumstance altogether.

He'd let go of the hammer – Flood, that is – and it had landed on its head on the floor next to his feet. Guy has told Alison this. She'll say he told her he thought it didn't look like blood leaching out across the hearth rug, it was more like oil leaking from a machine. Roseanne, he'd told Alison, had fallen into a particular position, as if she was listening hard to something coming up from the cellar, as if she had pressed her ear against the floor trying to hear, or as if she had fallen at Flood's feet in adoration. And Flood had let go of the hammer, let it drop and it had landed on its head, just there.

Guy had told Alison how Ivan was taking big gulps of air. 'Rose,' he said, and he'd reached across, placed his hand on the rise of her hip, his eye was so swollen it just looked like a fold in his face. 'Rose,' he said again. Guy had told her this, had said something about it sounding like the beginning of an incantation, or like a magic word. He'd told her how the coal in the fireplace seemed suddenly to have taken hold and was letting out ratty, spitty sounds and the room was coloured differently, slightly unreal, a painting, suddenly, one with no particular great flourish of artistry, one with no fussy business, no dazzling realism, no real regard for perspective or geometry. And Guy would have been sure he could smell the blood. Alison will tell all this.

And the details. She'll say there are details Guy told her, like how Derek stood, swaying gently, and that Roseanne was making a little sound and stretching her fingers out to the place on her head that looked, just then, like a smit mark. Guy, so he said – why would he say this? – noticed through the window a blackbird swoop down from a branch, and the slurp of water from a drain. And then this: a laugh coming from somewhere, but it was a laugh that didn't belong in that house, at that time, it belonged in a pub or a fairground. It was Donna, in her school uniform, her school bag on the floor next to the work boots in the hallway. Up until then, she didn't look her age. She wasn't tall, her skin was too white, her hair too baby-fine, but standing there, so Alison will say Guy told her, she looked quite suddenly ancient. And she would not stop laughing. He tried to move her away, to steer her out of this and away from this scene, but she was solid, planted right next to him, her eyes fixed on all this like she was watching a pantomime. And Flood turned to look at her, Donna, or at Guy, or both. This is what Alison will say she was told. This is the detail: light from the fire flickered, catching like a spark in Flood's eye. And he said something like, 'Shut up, or I'll gi' you one an' all.' And he was talking to them all. And the way he'd said it, it was unusual for such a huge, heavy, godlike man to speak so softly. And it was as if someone had flicked a switch, and Donna did shut up, and Alison will say Guy distinctly remembered hearing the way Donna's breath was catching, and looking back, remembering it, it sounded like when the wind blows up across the grass under the viaduct next to the river.

Alison will tell how Ivan was the one who said, 'Get an ambulance.' And there are little tiny details we might fill in, like the way Ivan's thumb, his fingers, might have been moving across Roseanne's forehead in repeated circles as if he was drawing a pattern or rubbing a lamp to try and release a genie, and how his fingers came away from her forehead glistening; like Roseanne's hair, its thick, coarse, layers, like strata, like the lie of the land, and her ear with a piercing in the lobe nobody had ever realised she had; perhaps there was a hangnail on her thumb and a cat scratch, say, on her bare left arm. And all of them, all five of them, looking at her like she was this strange, curious, beautiful thing.

And Alison will say she wishes - she would say this, of course - that she hadn't known this, she wishes she hadn't been told any of it. But she had been. And so have you, now.

∗

Alison will say it was like the earth was slipping sideways under her feet, and she'll say she clung onto Guy's hand. She'll say she *clung on*, yes, but it felt like she was holding nothing. The sun was a ball of blood sheathing the place in flickering red, setting behind a greasy mass of factories. She had an awful headache and she closed her eyes briefly, sure it would start off another migraine, but doing that just made her more aware of the smell of the place, of the smell of rot. She'll tell how she could hear her own heartbeat like a panting breath in her ears and how she didn't feel entirely in control of herself, of her legs, of her feet. She felt like she, they, she and Guy, were being absorbed by the landscape here, reduced to walking shadows. There was such a lack of energy. Beside them, the canal was a wide gaping mirror, and some plant, gnarled and brown, had taken over a brick wall on the opposite side. She'll tell how she could make out signs on it, graffiti that didn't make sense, not letters from an alphabet she knew: triangles, arrows, perhaps shapes that might have looked like a word. 'Hades', perhaps, is what she'll say.

Guy hesitated, but only for a second, as they rounded the bend near the old house and the metal grid of the weir, and Alison will tell how she saw his breath, dark, and she shivered. The woman, Donna - it was her - stood on the towpath ahead of them as if she was on the edge of something, and they approached her, like you might approach a frightened animal, or an angry one. Alison will explain how from that distance, looking at Donna, it was like looking at herself, a woman in transition. The landscape, too, was the same, moving between something unstable, punished by a mix of past and present, and fearful of the future.

'What the fuck are you doing?' He kept saying it, Guy did, so Alison will say, and he let go of her hand and she'll say it made her feel like she might suddenly float away like a bit of ash, and she stumbled, nearly fell. He looked at her and she'll say now that she felt somehow outfoxed by him, by the place, by herself, by everything. And he moved away from her, and she'll say she heard someone say his name – it was her, she said it – but that her mind was blank and the sound of her own voice made her tremble. Everything around her felt hard and dangerous, even the water – especially the water. Everything looked like it was in the process coming to an end, of dying on the stem, and that if she stayed there, if she didn't move, she knew she would too. But she'll say she watched him go, Guy, striding through the mud there, like he was walking through old footprints into which his fitted. She'll tell how she watched his walking reflection flicker across the surface of the wide water, a dark ghost. Donna seemed to step forward, or try to – she seemed to try to step forward off the towpath into, or maybe onto, the water. Alison will describe this, the way she balanced on one foot, balletically, her breath making thin shapes.

'Donna,' Guy called out, his voice like a boy's. He was running then, towards her, and she stopped. She stopped herself, Donna did, and turned to look at him, at them. And Alison will tell how she played out the scene, the alternative scene, a pre-emptive one, in her head: Donna falling into the water, the way her hair would splay out against the surface like an opening flower, the colour her skin would look, the way the weeds and debris might grab at her, the way the child might struggle in her grip. But across the canal, on the other side, there was movement. Alison will tell how she heard them before she saw them, the noise of what they were doing drifting across the surface of the water. It could have been stifled laughter, and it was only when she concentrated that she saw two people, a lad and a girl in amongst the saplings and dead wood against the bank there on the other side of the canal. A weak light from a factory flickered on and shone across them, lighting up the angles of shoulders and elbows – the machinery of them – almost indistinguishable against the backdrop. The girl was on her knees in front of the lad, his head tilted back slightly. Alison will say she thought his eyes were closed, or maybe he had no eyes, or perhaps it was that the scraps of light made the components of his face seem to dissolve. She'll say she can't be sure, but the girl's face seemed buried against him, thin hanks of her dark hair, just a black veil, and the sallow skin of the lad's hands against the back of her head were strong with anger. It was the gauntness of them both that was most shocking. But Alison will say there seemed to be a particular smell, just then and there, that she found oddly comforting. From somewhere, though, the sound of an explosion, or what could have been an explosion, or the sound of a fast car braking and then back-firing, made the sky crack open with colours, then sparks – more sounds than light, really, so Alison will say. It was a firework, and the life of it only lasted, what? Two seconds? Three? Hardly that. It scrawled an arc so brief in the sky behind the factories that the canal didn't even register it. But its impact seemed to make the place swell, the sensation of it. The potential of it was something to be felt, remembered, not described. It left behind a smell of stale gas of some kind, of something waiting for a match to happen. Alison will say when she looked back at the bank on the other side, the lad and the girl weren't there, perhaps they never had been, but the shape of the undergrowth, the way the branches of the saplings were, they looked like thin bodies, little skeletons. Just then, she'll say she thought, anyway, we're all just bones in the end. And she'll say Donna still stood, ahead, there, in front, and she looked at her and her face was little more than a skull. It was, Alison will say, as if the flesh of her was disappearing bit by bit. Guy had taken the child from her, was touching the soft spot on top of his head and the child looked at him like an obedient dog might. Alison will tell how she saw Guy saying something and imagined it was about how the funeral was later that day, how it wasn't the thing to be doing, going wandering off like that. She'll say his lips moved, she could see them, but the air still vibrated with tension all around them, that even the flow of the canal seemed suddenly different, suddenly febrile. When he walked towards her, Guy was holding the baby against his chest, his hand holding the back of its head, and she'll tell how they walked back along the towpath, Donna, Guy and the baby, ahead of her, that the surface of the water was stuttering in places against the wind or that air, that there was litter of a particular type blown away next to tree trunks and caught in amongst the weeds and that there were a couple of small, black polythene bags tied to shivering branches. Already the light was fading and the sky was a brownish scab. It would be blizzarding soon. She'll say she could feel it, the threat of it in the air. And she could hear them talking in front of her, talking and walking in front of her, that is, Donna and

Guy, but not what they were saying, exactly, just the pulse of their voices. And the baby peered at her over Guy's shoulder, she'll say, or maybe not peered, exactly, more just gave her the whale-eye, and she'll say that, to her, the way it, he, was being held, he looked like a scrimp of a being, just a growth of some kind, as if she could, if she wanted to, break his scrawny neck, or Guy could.

And it seemed like a long walk back – longer than before. Her feet hurt from it. And the sky had turned crimson over the town, and a flock of grey birds wheeled over the swell of the housing estate. Alison will say there was a shift in scale that dwarfed Guy, Donna and that baby against the rise of the path. She'll say she remembers noticing how they never actually touched each other, Guy and Donna, yet they were walking almost entirely in step, keeping whatever was between them in a thin slice of dark air, just there. And they were walking so quickly, she'll say there was a sense that she couldn't keep up with them. Perhaps she was tired, exhausted, Alison, but she'll only say her legs felt heavy, her feet dragged, water had seeped into her boots. As the towpath ended, the earth around her looked like a series of shallow graves, and she'll say she thought that must have been a different route back to the farm, surely. Nothing looked familiar to her. She didn't recognise the empty factories, the housing estate. She'll say she'd slowed her pace by then, was wandering, or felt like she was. She'll say that from where she was, it looked cluttered, medieval, the landscape did, everything outlined in black – reduced to a child's drawing. She'll talk about how the row of semi-detached houses there all seemed to have black windows, and there was a hand-painted sign – white paint daubed onto hardboard leaning up against wire fencing – that said 'Not God Dont Go.' And she'll tell how the street was deserted but for a child's scooter, one wheel missing, and how a streetlight flickered, and she realised she'd lost sight of them, Guy and Donna and the child. There was a turn they could have taken, to the left, so she took it, hoping that some kind of homing instinct might kick in. The footpath, she'll say, shimmered, wet, the camber of it strange, and she watched her own feet quicken up like they were part of someone else's body, or a dismembered part of hers, like she was watching a film. She'll say she reached the subway that goes under the ring-road. Something about the quality of light there made her feel drugged, or that she was going blind, and the air was so cold against her face, she'll say it felt like acid. There were a couple of bent shopping trollies having been left pushed up against the sprigs of laurel bushes, and as she walked through, she'll tell how she realised there were no cars about, no people either, no sounds at all. There were lights on in some of the factories in the industrial estate though, and walking up, alongside the road, she'll say it made that dip there, full of workshops and lean-to units, look like a big bowl of glitter, and the thought occurred to her then that this place is a just composite of enchantment and despair. Litter and broken glass lined the dual carriageway and she'll tell how she realised her breath made a trail, but her footfall was silent. Ahead of her, the viaduct, was, to her, a monstrosity of black bricks and graffiti that kept disappearing. The closer she ought to have been getting to it, the further away it seemed to become. She'll tell how she realised she was feeling no sense of time or distance any more, like, she'll say, the cognitive edgeland of a feeling between decisions, or in the midst of a change of heart. She'll tell how, between her and the factories, the culvert flowed, and the sense of sudden movement somehow made it all seem more intense, worse. The smell of the river was like cheap perfume and she followed it, across the road, into the field she thought she recognised. Her boots sank into the rotten ground in a way that could have made her think she was in danger of being swallowed up, but the sheerness of feeling was more like flying through space. The sun must have been somewhere there but she'll tell how, in that light, the uneven ground looked like bodies and made it seem like a long way across the field. She'll say she was drawn to the shadows and was beginning to lose hope that she would ever get out, but when a wedge of dark birds uptilted right in front of her, it seemed like they sent a wave of something at her. The sense of updraught along the valley there made her stop still, and she'll say she felt just like a speck of something, nothing more important than that. She'll say she hadn't realised the river ran alongside the field, and she could see it, quite still, a floating wound, lined with clusters of Giant Hogweed. Ahead, the viaduct was closer then, of course, and without warning, she saw something moving along the top. A train, gliding like a serpent, a slow, suspicious creep. She'll tell how she watched it and realised it was a goods train, and it moved, pulling carriage after carriage, labouring, not so much floating as fading past, and the valley there below seemed to gasp for breath. Ask her how long all this took and she won't know for sure, but she'll say her feet were soaking wet by then, she couldn't even feel them, and she'll say she had to struggle to walk on, under the viaduct, where black mould and decay blurred the bricks under the arch there, where she'll say the train still hissed and she'll tell how there was something white in the curve above her, and she'd thought it might have been graffiti or that perhaps there were bones there, buried somewhere in the bricks. And she'll say there was a gust of cold air, and it smelled of something particular that she recognised, that she felt close to but can't describe. It smelled of Guy. And she'll say she knew then that the farm wasn't far off. She'll say her skin felt odd, prickling, like the onset of a fever as she walked on, past the low-rise blocks of flats, unlit, past the industrial units that looked, to her, derelict. She'll say she felt lost, out of place, her head was aching, she wanted to cry but couldn't conjure tears. Instead, all her senses were sharpened so that her clothes felt heavy against her, and her thoughts did. Something about the evolutionary pressure bearing down on the place was an agony. She'll say she knew she was creeping, like a criminal, that the smell of wet concrete was being slowly replaced by the smell of smoke and rot. She must have looked pathetic, like a drunk, as she wandered off towards the hill, towards where she thought the farm was, and as if some internal magnetic mechanism was working, she'll say she saw it, the farm, up there on the horizon, a shadow stirring. She'll tell how she could see the fall of lambs and followed the gape of the lane upwards.

And this is what she'll say: that the caravan at the top there in the yard looked slightly out of true, its door open, the just-about sight of an unmade bed. She'll say she stopped to look, and all she could hear just then was her own breathing, wheezing as if with illness; that the air held traces of animal, the musk of them; that ahead of her she could see there were puddles in the yard forming blisters in the concrete; that the dry-stone wall along the side there stood like a row of broken teeth. And then, she'll say she saw him, Guy, in an upstairs window. He'd put on a light and was looking out, but she doesn't know or won't say if it was at her, or for her. She'll say this though, that something about him wasn't right. The way he stood, and that his skin looked stone-coloured, his face a slightly different shape. She'll say now, that only then did it occur to her that he might be ill. Downstairs, someone had lit a candle and it flickered on the window sill, and someone shouted something, or perhaps an animal cried out. She stumbled as she approached the yard, because she still couldn't feel her feet, but she'll say she knew that the hummocky sand and gravel overburdening the ashes of bodies of those gone before, buried in haste, and the coal mines were far too dangerous for her to know about. She'll say she imagined Guy and Ivan playing here in this lane, in this yard, in these fields and woods, perhaps, hiding and seeking, perhaps building secret dens, finding secret paths and passages, doing secret things – things so secret, even she wasn't told about them. And when she looked, she'll say she imagined their footprints, but not hers, not just yet. And the closer she got to the farm, the more she'll have thought how easy it might be to hide here, and never be found. And she'll tell how the sky suddenly looked huge – one long sigh above the farm, above this place, here. Something about the universe was changing, some cosmic chance or celestial show, as if before an eclipse or a divine event. She didn't understand it then. She didn't understand that's how it is here, not then. She took one look back, so she'll say. The horizon, suddenly clear, contoured with housing estates and treed hills that didn't look real. And she'll tell how she saw the tower blocks, and the factories, and the spire of a church, and the mount, risen like a volcano behind it. And, even from that distance, she'll say she saw it, of course she did, a glint of metal at the summit of that mount. And she'll say now, she realised then why this was God's Country. A mist was drifting down from the farm, swelling like a current around her feet, out across the field, through gaps in the trees and out over the river, an apparition, escaping. She'll tell how a panic of dark birds rose up over the field and scattered, and perhaps she imagined, just for a very intense moment, walking away. But she wouldn't admit to that. All that she'll say she was thinking is that this place is more expressive than any of the people in it, that this place has its own mentality. She's right. See, she felt it then, the sensation of it. You might be moving, wandering about, but it, this place here, seems to stay still in time and movement, seems to hold you within it, and that's powerful. Godlike.

She'll tell how she had to push hard at the door of the farm to open it. Inside, it was colder, and she'll say she grabbed a coat from the hanger, one of Guy's, and put it on over hers. And she'll tell how she called to him, Guy. She called his name. And then she called to him again.

# ACKNOWLEDGEMENTS

THIS IS A novel that has been simmering inside me for years, I think it contains part of my own DNA. *God's Country* is where I am from, it's the paths I have walked, and I am massively indebted to Paul Evans and Tina Richardson, and to Nicholas Royle, who, as well as being my friend and encourager, introduced me to Chris and Jen Hamilton-Emery at the wonderful Salt Publishing, and I am very grateful for their support and kindness. My love and hearty respect goes to my inspirational Moniack Mhor writing friends whose support is unerring. I'm lucky to have such a patient and supportive family, for whom thanks doesn't seem enough. And the Black Country, *God's Country*, I thank you.

# ACKNOWLEDGMENTS

This book has been typeset by
SALT PUBLISHING LIMITED
using Neacademia, a font designed by Sergei Egorov
for the Rosetta Type Foundry in the Czech Republic. It
is manufactured using Holmen Book Cream 70gsm, a
Forest Stewardship Council™ certified paper from the
Hallsta Paper Mill in Sweden. It was printed and bound
by Clays Limited in Bungay, Suffolk, Great Britain.

CROMER
GREAT BRITAIN
MMXXIII